Books by Valerie Worth

GYPSY GOLD

GYPSY GOLD
Valerie Worth

Farrar Straus Giroux · New York

For Natalie Babbitt

Contents

(vii)

GYPSY GOLD

n one of the cobbled streets of an ancient market town there stood an apothecary's shop, its entrance overhung by two quaintly timbered upper storeys, the whole house built high and narrow between its neighbors.

This shop, and the living quarters above it, had been handed on from father to son for generations. Successive proprietors, gaining some local renown for their powders and salves and elixirs, had grown increasingly solemn and pale and respectable, and their wives, as well as their children, inclined to the same sober traits.

Yet one less prudent heir ventured to marry a lively redheaded beauty, and in time a daughter was born to them, endowed with her mother's fiery hair, though her eyes were like her father's, a deep brown. This exceptional marriage might have turned out well enough in itself; but unfortunately, as the years went by, it became apparent that the couple's daughter was to be an only child, so that for the first time since its establishment there would be no son to carry on the family business.

The apothecary was mortified, and privately blamed his rash choice of a wife for this awkward state of affairs. While he tried to persuade himself that a daughter, even one with red hair, might still be taught the work of the shop, he continued to brood over the matter, and went about looking paler and gloomier than ever.

The child, called Miranda after a lately deceased

grandmother, grew up sturdy and hale, with a wealth of bright if highly refractory curls. Miranda was of a warm-hearted disposition, eager to please, and crestfallen when she failed to do so—the latter all too frequently the case, as she tended to act with impetuous haste and end in a muddle. Nevertheless, the apothecary clung to his hopes of training the girl in his own line of work; and once she had reached an appropriate age, he began her instruction.

But although she tried her best, Miranda was far from a ready pupil, nor was her father a patient teacher, and often their sessions lapsed into scoldings and tears, especially in regard to Miranda's impulsive ways, which made her so clumsy that even the simple task of pouring a fluid from one container to another was apt to result in disaster.

The apothecary, his long, bony fingers always so quick and precise, was driven to near-distraction by Miranda's fumblings among his precious vials and flasks; and after a fruitless year or so, bitterly disappointed, he pronounced his daughter a dunce and banished her from the shop, saying that since she was clearly fit for nothing better she must be educated by her mother in sewing and cookery instead.

Miranda was downcast, and suffered a lingering sense of shame, unhappily not to be eased by her mother's lessons. For her fingers proved just as inept at darning and hem-stitching as they had at measuring ounces and drams and scruples; while her attempts to separate an egg, or merely to boil one, led to as many mishaps as had her dealings with delicate glassware.

Even her mother began to despair of turning Miranda into a capable housewife, let alone an apothecary; and late one night she sat down with her husband and spoke to him seriously about their daughter's future.

"The girl may be slow, but she's pretty enough," she said. "A little too plump, perhaps, but that can be remedied; and I believe the only answer's to find her a wealthy husband. With a houseful of servants and no need ever to lift a finger, she'd make an agreeable wife, if not a very useful one."

"I suppose you're right," conceded the apothecary glumly. "But who's to inherit the shop, then, if she marries a man already successful at something else?"

"I've thought of that, too," his wife replied. "Why not take on your sister's boy as an apprentice? He's a likely lad, for all your sister's brought him up as an awful prig; and if he does well, you can leave the shop to him. I'm sure Miranda wouldn't object, if she'd a husband with money of his own."

After some thought, the apothecary consented to this scheme, and applied himself forthwith to seeking out a wealthy match for Miranda, as well as drawing up an apprenticeship for his nephew, an ambitious youth of seventeen; which turn of events suited the boy and his widowed mother to perfection.

Told nothing as yet of her fate, Miranda felt only relief when her domestic lessons were discontinued, although she was left with little to do, and passed much of her time drifting aimlessly about the house or gazing dreamily out of the window into the street below. As an antidote to these languid habits, her mother began to insist on Miranda's walking with her every afternoon to the park, or to the market square, or up and down the busy streets; and Miranda herself found the sights of the town a welcome diversion, especially the market's weekly congregation of farmers and peddlers and gypsies, whose unknown lives invested even the humblest of them with a certain romance.

The gypsies in particular caught her fancy, not only their swarthy skin and colorful dress, but the notion of their adventurous wanderings—compared to which Miranda's own existence seemed to her woefully dull and confined, and often provoked her to reveries of maidens imprisoned in lonely towers and gallant knights who rode to their deliverance.

In any event, thanks to these daily walks, Miranda did grow slimmer, and was fitted for some stylish dresses to replace the simpler clothing of her childhood. Her complexion improved, her wayward curls yielded to a more decorous arrangement, and all in all, by the time Miranda turned sixteen, and the apothecary confided to his wife that he had discovered a promising match for the girl, she might well have gladdened any suitor's eye.

An introduction was planned, and Miranda, arrayed in her most becoming gown for the occasion, grew attractively flushed at the prospect of dining with, as she supposed, some new and interesting acquaintance of her parents'.

If she was quieter than usual throughout the evening, still she answered with due civility when spoken to. But secretly Miranda found her parents' dinner guest a great disappointment, and wondered how they had ever come to make friends with this boorish old fellow, who talked of nothing but sheep and cloth, while at intervals grinning and winking at her in the most ludicrous fashion.

The party drew to an end at last, and their guest went away all smiles, having squeezed Miranda's hand with exceeding benevolence—though she could not help thinking his own hand lamentably moist and doughy. But even when Miranda's father summoned her to him the following night, saying that he wished to consult her on an important matter, she suspected nothing. And when he inquired, to begin with, how she had liked their recent visitor, Miranda replied in complete innocence that she had thought him very silly, and not in the least handsome.

Her father reproved her, saying she must not speak so of her elders. But then, with another attempt at diplomacy, he told Miranda that she had made a most favorable impression on the kind gentleman—so favorable, in fact, that he had made her an offer of marriage.

Miranda stared at him, wide-eyed. "Father, you must be joking," she exclaimed. "Why, I'd sooner marry the chimney sweep than that ridiculous old man!"

In spite of himself, the apothecary lost his temper. "It's not a matter of your preferences, my girl," he said with asperity. "You can't expect to loll about at home forever; and who else do you think will have you, when you've not learned a mortal thing about housekeeping? But come now," he went on more calmly, "he's not so old, scarcely fifty, and he's made a sizable fortune in the wool trade. You wouldn't do better if you waited another ten years."

"Then I'll wait twenty!" rejoined Miranda, spurred to unwonted rebellion. "But I won't be wed to the likes of him!" And so saying, she burst into tears.

Failing to stem their flow by further admonition, her father threw up his hands and walked from the room. He was a good deal taken aback by Miranda's response, as she had always behaved with perfect docility in the past; but when he reported the result of this interview to his wife, she simply laughed.

"I'll talk to her myself," she said. "It's more the idea of leaving home than anything else, I expect."

She went off to Miranda's room, where the girl was lying on the bed, still tearful; and sitting down at her side, she began to speak in a soothing voice. "Now, now, my dear, your father and I only want what's best for you. Why, you'll be a fine lady, with a house of your own, and a carriage, and nothing to do but amuse yourself from morning to night. Just think it over for a day or two, and see if you don't agree."

Miranda, staring up at the ceiling with reddened eyes,

made no reply; so after a little time her mother gave her hand a parting pat and left her alone.

Once she had gone, Miranda got up and walked restlessly about, twisting her handkerchief in her fingers and trying to compose herself. In truth, and somewhat to her surprise, she was less unhappy than angry, more so than ever in her life before. "They only want to be rid of me," she said to herself. "It's not for my sake, but their own. They've made up their minds I'm good for nothing at home, so they'll send me off to be a burden to somebody else—but I won't be treated so, I won't!" And Miranda tossed her head in defiance, looking very much like her mother at that moment.

"Still," she reflected more soberly, "they'll never forgive me if I refuse, and that'll mean living on in this dreary house with both of them set against me. I suppose I could run away, if I had any money—but there's only my birthday sovereign, and besides, where should I go? I couldn't just wander about, and nobody'd take me in—except the gypsies, perhaps. Oh! I wonder if they would! They're always traveling here and there, and I could go off with them and never come home again. And gypsies have such a lovely life, singing and dancing and telling fortunes. I could wear a kerchief, and earrings— and perhaps they'd show me how to tell fortunes myself!"

Miranda flushed pink with excitement, almost forgetting her former anger. But then her spirits fell anew; for it was highly unlikely that she could slip away from her mother to speak to those gypsies who came to the market,

(9)

and how should she meet them otherwise, since they vanished again after market day and kept to their caravans, hidden in some remote lane or field where she might never find them.

All the same, there was something heartening about this vision of the gypsies and their carefree ways; and she vowed to herself, as at last she made ready for bed, that if her life at home became unendurable she would seek them out somehow, and beg them to take her along with them into the world: where some happier destiny might lie waiting for her even now.

ext morning, going straight to her father, Miranda informed him that she had thought over the gentleman's proposal, and decided once and for all that she could not accept it.

The apothecary grew angrier still, and called in his wife to witness Miranda's obstinacy for herself.

"I'm sorry," Miranda appealed to the two of them, "I don't mean to be contrary; but if only you'll let me try to do better at housekeeping, I'm sure I can make a good wife to some nicer husband, if not such a rich one."

"Oh no, my girl," her mother objected. "We'll not begin that nonsense over again. Either you marry as your father and I wish, or you stay at home in idleness; please yourself. But if you're to stop here, I'll have nothing more to do with you—nor, I expect, will your father, for we've both reached the end of our patience."

"Your mother's right," her father asserted coldly. "Unless you come to your senses, I wash my hands of you from this day forth." And he turned and strode out of the room.

"Ah, Miranda," her mother resumed in gentler tones, "won't you think better of it? You've time to change your mind—run after your father now, there's a dear girl, and say you'll do as you're told."

"No, Mother, I can't, and I won't," Miranda replied, with a look in her eye that her mother had never seen before. "Though I'll be very sorry if you and Father care nothing about me any longer." And with a sudden change of countenance, she ran from the room, leaving her mother more than ever astonished.

Neither the apothecary nor his wife had dreamed that Miranda would prove so resolute. But now, like it or not, they were obliged to stand by their harsh threats, and after that day took it upon themselves to behave as though Miranda were no longer a member of their household.

While she joined them at meals, they spoke not a word to her, and the rest of the time the poor girl might have been invisible. She dressed as she liked, got up and went to bed when she chose, and for a week or so even took a mutinous pleasure in these liberties; yet, as the days went by, she wearied of the silence and isolation thrust upon her, and grew both indignant and miserable once more.

Those cheerless days came to weigh heavily on her parents as well; and it is not improbable that if events had been left to themselves, Miranda might have been forgiven in the end. But after less than a fortnight, it chanced that Miranda, gazing dispiritedly through the window at the bustle of the street below, remembered that it was market day, and thought again of her reckless vow to run away with the gypsies—which had continued to lurk at the back of her mind, if only as a melancholy fancy rather than any well-formed scheme.

Today, however, unable to bear the tedious gloom of the house a moment longer, she deliberated, and made a plan of sorts. Knotting up her birthday sovereign in a handkerchief, and changing her gown for an old skirt and plain calico bodice, she threw on a shawl and slipped out into the street.

Never before had Miranda walked through the town by herself. But this afternoon, emboldened by desperation, she took her way alone to the marketplace, where farmers and tradesmen had set up row upon row of stalls, their counters heaped with fruits and vegetables, kettles and crockery, ribbons and sweets and frivolous trinkets, all in the midst of a cheerfully noisy throng.

Miranda wandered about for some time, pausing to admire a string of beads here, and a lace collar there—at the same time edging slowly towards that far side of the square where a handful of gypsies was usually to be found. Though, when at length she came in sight of their barrow, her courage failed, and she stopped short, affecting to study a china shepherdess at a nearby stall.

From this vantage point she could hear the gypsies recommending their stock of baskets and willow hampers to passersby. Glancing in their direction every so often, she noted that today there were only three of them: a young man, an older woman, and a child of some three or four years, all with the same dark skin and black curling hair, but dressed in rather a sorry assortment of patched and faded garments.

They were not, in reality, much as she had imagined them, or thought she had remembered them—perhaps misled by a picture in one of her childhood books, which had shown a band of gypsies dancing beside a fire, decked out in velvets and silks, and brightly adorned with necklaces and earrings. True, this woman wore gold hoops in her ears, and a flowered kerchief tied over her head, while the child, a boy, was buttoned up in an oversized jacket made of some worn stuff that might have been velvet once; but otherwise these three looked distinctly impoverished, and even, perhaps, ill-fed.

In some respects, however, their shabbiness daunted her less than a display of gaudy finery might have done; so at last she moved towards them, feeling their eyes upon her as she drew near.

"Will you buy something today, miss?" inquired the woman, as Miranda halted before the barrow and picked up a little straw basket as if to inspect it more closely. "That one's just right to hold your ribbons or handkerchiefs, and only fourpence—or see this other, it's even nicer, for just a penny more."

At first Miranda could not think how to respond. But raising her eyes to meet the woman's—and the young man's and the boy's as well, as all three regarded her with mild curiosity—she finally burst out, "Please, I don't really want a basket, but I wonder if you know how to tell fortunes?"

"Ah, it's that, is it?" said the woman, smiling. "I might have known. Pretty girls always want to hear about their sweethearts—and why shouldn't they, to be sure?"

Miranda stood silent, confused and embarrassed. Yet she liked the sound of this woman's voice, which had a musical rise and fall to it, almost as if she sang a little while she talked; and though her accent was unfamiliar, her manner was neither outlandish nor mysterious, but surprisingly down-to-earth.

"But you see, dear," the woman went on, in lower tones, "it's not so easy nowadays. We daren't tell fortunes openly, unless it's at a fair, or an entertainment where we're hired for the purpose—and even then there's some don't think it's right. No, you'd have to visit us at the caravans, where nobody's about to mind. I'm sorry to disappoint you, but you'll understand how it is."

"Yes, of course," Miranda replied. "But you see, that isn't quite what I meant. I thought you might teach me how to tell fortunes myself. If I paid you for it," she added hastily, observing the woman's startled expression.

"Indeed, miss," the woman declared, "that's a queer thing to ask. How ever did you come to think of it? Why, fortune-telling's a matter for those born to it, not a young lady such as yourself. You'd best forget about it altogether, or only play at it with the other girls, for a lark."

"Oh dear," Miranda mourned, tears springing to her eyes. "I did want to learn something of the sort, so I could ask you to take me along with you. That's what I'd really like, for I've left home, and I've nowhere else to go. But if you took me in, I'd do anything—not fortunes, then, but washing, or fetching water—anything at all, to earn my keep." And in the midst of her entreaty, Miranda began to weep in earnest.

"Well, I never!" exclaimed the gypsy, confounded by this exhibition. "Now see here, miss," she said firmly at last, while Miranda, sniffing, fumbled in her pocket for her handkerchief, "you'd much better go straight home before you find yourself in trouble—or get us into trouble ourselves. There's already tales enough of gypsies stealing children, and we can't afford another. Besides, it wouldn't do for a girl of your sort, you'd soon see. You'd be off like a hare to your mother and father before a week was out."

"I wouldn't," returned Miranda stubbornly, drying her eyes on her knotted handkerchief. "I'm strong, and willing to work, though they don't believe it at home. Oh, won't you please try me? See, I've got some money, and you can have it to pay my way." Quickly untying her handkerchief, she held out the gold sovereign on her palm.

The little boy looked at it with interest, although the young man appeared to take scant notice of this curious conversation. The woman, however, closed Miranda's fingers about the coin, and said to her gently, "Put your money away, my dear. It's no use asking—we couldn't take you with us even if we'd a mind to. Now hurry along home, it'll soon be dark, and it's time we were leaving ourselves."

She gave Miranda's hand a kindly pat, but afterwards turned aside, so that the unhappy girl was given no chance to argue further. The young man avoided her eyes, although the little boy continued to stare at her in some fascination.

While Miranda stood by, forlorn, the gypsy woman spoke quietly to the others, and they set about packing up their wares and covering over the barrow with a weather-stained canvas. Then, without another word, they moved away, the woman and boy in front, and the young man pushing the barrow behind.

But as Miranda gazed after them, the young man turned briefly to look back at her; and his face, which throughout the former proceedings had remained expressionless, broke into a smile: not a smile of mockery, as might have been expected, but one of uncommon sweetness, as though he had understood Miranda's disappointment, and would have consoled her if he could. And for an instant, as his thin, dark face was illuminated by that fleeting smile, he took on such an uncanny resemblance to the gypsies in Miranda's picture book that she was very much tempted to run after the three departing figures and plead her cause once more.

The next moment, however, she thought better of it. She waited, instead, until they were nearly out of sight; and only then did she start off cautiously in the same direction. Night was fast falling, and she had little difficulty in following unseen, though once the young man glanced over his shoulder again and Miranda was obliged to dart into the shadows of a doorway. But after that none of the three looked back; and before long they had made their way out of the town, taking a road that wound towards the nearest village.

Having traveled along it for a short stretch, they turned abruptly into a narrow lane, nearly hidden by overgrown hedgerows. Miranda might have missed the turning altogether, had it not been for the murmur of the gypsies' voices and the creaking of the barrow, which she pursued now rather than any visible sign of their progress.

The autumn night was very clear and growing much colder. Miranda shivered beneath her shawl no matter how closely she drew it about her, and the half-frozen mud of the lane crept in through the soles of her shoes. She was thankful, then, to hear the gypsies more distinctly as they slowed their steps to push the barrow through a gap in the hedge.

After a pause, Miranda followed through the same ragged opening, to find herself at the edge of a wide starlit field. Some distance across it burned a campfire, near which some four or five caravans stood ranged, while off to one side moved the shadowy figures of several horses.

She drew back into the hedge again, for she could see her three gypsies clearly as they trundled the barrow up to the fire. They were soon joined by a number of others, emerging from the caravans to greet them; then something was ladled out of a pot, and everyone sat down on the ground to eat.

Forced to wait motionless in her hiding place, Miranda grew colder than ever. Now that she had discovered the gypsies' camp, she felt rather at a loss, and even began to regret her foolhardy adventure. But presently, having finished their meal, the gypsies one after another withdrew inside the caravans, until the fire flickered deserted, and all was still except for the occasional stamp and snuffle of the horses.

So Miranda stole away from the hedge at last, treading

silently over the frosty grass towards the fire. She could sense its warmth on her face as she drew near, and felt some of her courage restored by its generous influence. But in stooping down to the low flames, she overbalanced; and as she threw herself backwards to keep from tumbling into the coals, her hand fell against a stack of tin plates left nearby, knocking them over with a clatter.

At once there started up a fearful row from beneath one of the caravans, where a dog was chained. The door was flung open, and a man descended the steps, shouting, "Hold your noise, Bruno! What's amiss, then?"

The next moment he caught sight of Miranda, risen to her feet beside the fire. "How's this?" demanded the gypsy, striding over to her. "What are you about, missy? Now then, speak up—you've no business here, and you'd better explain yourself."

Miranda only stood mute, looking into the man's rough, dark face with frightened eyes. By now the other gypsies were roused as well, and a number of them came hastening out to see what was the matter.

"Heaven help us, it's that girl," exclaimed someone in the little crowd gathering about Miranda; and the woman she knew pushed forward, to gaze on her in consternation. "How ever did you find us?" she asked. "Here, Tom, I've seen her before—we were talking earlier, at the market."

Drawing the man aside, she spoke to him rapidly in a low voice. His face hardened while she did so, and when she had finished, he turned back to Miranda with a scowl.

"Thought you'd run off with the gypsies, is it?" he

said. "Well, now you must think again. They'd be coming to look for you in the morning, if they're not on their way already. But that's not the worst of it—for do you have any notion of what you've done? You've as much as driven us out, that's how it is. We must pack up and go this very night or have the law on us, saying we tried to steal you away.

"As for you, my girl," he continued, more harshly still, "you'll take yourself off this minute. You came here somehow, and you can go back the same road—and if you were my daughter, you'd meet with a good thrashing when you got home!"

At the outset of this tirade, Miranda had shrunk back, not only afraid, but remorseful. But when, in the end, the gypsy ordered her to be gone, it was almost as though her own father were speaking those angry words; and Miranda felt the blood rush hot to her face.

She had refused to be banished by her parents, and she would not be sent away now. "No, I can't go home, and I won't!" she retorted, although her heart pounded wildly at her own daring. "I came to ask for your help, and I want to stay with you, even if you must leave tonight. I've some money, and I'll pay you to take me along. But if you won't, I'll say I was brought here against my will —and then you'll be in worse trouble than ever."

While Miranda spoke, the gypsy's expression had grown increasingly fierce; and all at once, before she knew what he was about, he stepped forward and struck her across the face.

She staggered back, raising her arm to ward off a further

blow; but the others held the gypsy fast. "Mercy on us, Tom, you've done it now," cried the woman. "You can never send her home with a mark like that!"

Putting a hand to her cheek, Miranda felt the warmth of blood moisten her fingers. She stared at her hand for a moment, while the gypsies waited in shocked silence to see what she would do. But then, amazingly, Miranda smiled; and said in a weak but triumphant voice, "It's true, isn't it? They'd never believe you after this, no matter what you told them."

"By God, the girl's a devil," muttered the gypsy man, shaking the others off. "What do you want of us, then?" he said, less savagely, but glaring at her still. "How do you think you'll live if you come with us? Who's to feed and clothe you—as if we hadn't worry enough looking out for ourselves? Besides, there's not a corner to hide you in, let alone an empty bed."

"Stay, Tom, I'll find room if she's to go," offered the woman, with a quick, kindly glance at Miranda. "But if she is, let's be off all the sooner, for they'll surely come searching for her here, and we'd better be well away by morning."

So in the end, grumbling and glowering, the gypsy allowed Miranda to be led away towards the caravans, while the others, standing aside, regarded her in greater wonder than ever. But Miranda saw in their midst the same young man who had turned and smiled at her earlier. And though he was not smiling now, his dark eyes shone; and he gave a slight nod as she passed, in what seemed almost a gesture of congratulation.

hatever next?" sighed the gypsy woman, leading Miranda up the steps of her caravan. "Though we've got through troubles before, and I expect we'll find our way past this one. What's your name, then, dear? Miranda—that's pretty. Mine's Dulcetta, but everyone calls me Dulcie," she said, preceding Miranda into a tiny room crowded with built-in bunks and cupboards, a small wood stove, and even a mirrored dresser with candle brackets at either side; while sundry bags and baskets hung from hooks about the walls.

"There's three of us live here," she went on. "Myself and my sister, Rosa, and her boy, Jemmy—he was the little one with me at the market. Rosa and I both lost our husbands some years ago, in a fire, but we needn't speak of that. I've a grown son, Leo, he was there at the market, too; though he stays in another caravan with my brother Tom, the one who was so rough with you just now.

"Tom's not a hard man, really," she added apologetically, "but he's got the rest of us to think about, and worries of his own, besides. Well, as you see, we've not much room, but we'll make do somehow, if you're willing to sleep on the floor."

Dulcie, meanwhile, was moving about the narrow space, fetching out blankets, and taking from a cupboard some remnants of bread and cheese. "I daresay you'll be hungry," she said. "You must have followed us straight from the market. Ah, but you are a silly girl, to be sure. And

I wouldn't have believed the way you spoke to Tom—though it seems you've got the better of him for the time being." Her lips twitched into a faint smile, in spite of herself.

Accepting her meager supper with gratitude, Miranda sat down on one of the bunks to eat, while Dulcie poured water from a pitcher into a basin, and wrung out a cloth to bathe Miranda's cheek. "It'll be coming up a fine bruise," she said, cleaning the blood away, "but the skin's only a little broken; you'll be good as new in a few days. Still, I hope you won't be so brazen with Tom again. In fact, it might be better if you kept out of his way at first."

Miranda looked up at her, chastened. "You've been very kind to me, Dulcie," she said. "I know I don't deserve it, but I thank you all the same. It was mainly your doing that I was allowed to stay, wasn't it? I wonder"—and she hesitated shyly before she went on—"are you the queen of the gypsies?"

Dulcie smiled without reserve at this. "Nay, we haven't kings or queens among us here," she answered. "Though there's others elsewhere may call themselves so. But we've not seen much of our own people for a number of years now, not since Tom quarreled with our elder brother, and some of us set off by ourselves. No, Tom wouldn't fancy himself a king, though he's generally the one to speak for us; and sometimes he'll listen to me, or to his wife—except Nan's so often ill. Then there's Nan's mother, too, that's Bella; she's older and wiser than any of us, but she'd only laugh if you said she was our queen.

"So you'd far better forget those gypsy tales you've got into your head," she told Miranda emphatically. "We're plain enough folk ourselves, with hard work just finding a spot to make camp, and earning what's needed to keep body and soul together. That's one reason Tom was so angry, because we'd fared better here than in many a place we've stopped. Still, if you'll mind your tongue and do as you're bid, perhaps he'll come round—but don't think you won't be set to work like the rest of us."

"But that's exactly what I'd hoped for," Miranda insisted.

"Well, then, we'll begin tonight," replied Dulcie. "There's Rosa coming back, and she'll want Jemmy put straight to bed. Here, Rosa," she said, as another woman entered with the child, "Miranda's going to look after Jemmy while we see to the packing up."

Rosa, younger and prettier than her sister, merely gave Miranda a sullen glance, and sat down wearily on one of the bunks. "My word, Dulcie, Tom's in a rage," she said. "I've left him flinging the harness about, and shouting at the dog and the horses; and Nan too ill to do anything with him." She cast another dark look in Miranda's direction.

"He's best left alone for now," Dulcie advised. "Just come and help me bring up the barrow and fetch in that washing from the line. Now then, Jemmy," she said, turning to the boy, "it's time for Miranda to tuck you into bed."

Jemmy only stared at Miranda dubiously, and refused

to be coaxed from his mother's side. Miranda at first hung back herself; but then, struck by a thought, she said, "Here, Jemmy, I've something in my pocket to show you."

Bringing out her handkerchief, she took from its folds the gold sovereign; and at last the child moved towards her. "It's pretty, isn't it?" she said to him. "And I'll let you keep it tonight—though it's really meant for your Aunt Dulcie, and you must give it to her in the morning."

The sisters exchanged a glance. Then Dulcie remarked, "I think you'd do better offering your money to Tom, my dear, than to anyone else. Though I'd wait till you've been with us longer. Perhaps he'll think of it as paying your keep, if you're to stay."

"Then Jemmy shall have it instead—only you must take care not to lose it," Miranda said to the boy, placing the coin in his hand. "Just you look after it until it's wanted again."

Rosa got up from the bunk. "You'll see to him, then?" she asked Miranda in a curt voice.

"Oh yes, we'll do nicely," said Miranda. "Come along, Jemmy, and when you're in bed I'll show you how to make a rabbit out of my handkerchief."

The sisters went away; and before long, knotting her handkerchief into a rabbit-like shape to amuse the boy, Miranda heard sounds of the barrow being fastened on to the caravan, and the clank of pails and kettles hung up beneath. Jemmy soon fell asleep, clutching both the coin and the handkerchief, and a little silence ensued. Then there came a tap at the door, and the young man Leo put in his head.

"Mother's not here?" he inquired.

"She's gone with your aunt to bring in some washing, I think," Miranda answered him, flustered, and rising to her feet.

Leo stood on in the doorway. "Are you all right, then?" he asked. "Tom fetched you a fair wallop, didn't he?"

"It's not as bad as it looked," Miranda replied, "and I suppose I deserved it. Besides, it's worth it to be going along with you—with all of you," she amended swiftly, and blushed in spite of herself.

"Aye, that's worth a good bit," Leo said with a slow smile, adding further to Miranda's confusion. But the next moment he turned away, saying, "Tell Mother I'll soon be along with the horse."

"What a fright I must look, though," Miranda muttered when he had gone. Moving over to the glass, she saw that one side of her face was appreciably swollen, while her hair stood out in a tangled mass about her head; and she wondered even more what Leo must have thought of her, despite his show of friendly concern.

"Of course he was just being kind," she told herself. "But I do wish I'd worn one of my new gowns." Then she turned away guiltily from the mirror, as the sisters came in, carrying a basket of plates and mugs and spoons, and a heap of clothing roughly folded.

"Leo was here," Miranda told Dulcie. "He said he'd be bringing the horse round."

"I'll go and help him," Dulcie replied with a nod, "and, Rosa, you see to things inside. But first give Miranda something else to put on, in case they come looking for her—and cover up that hair!"

She hurried out again, and Rosa began sorting through the pile of clothes she had laid on the bed. "I suppose you'd better have this skirt of mine," she said grudgingly. "You're taller than I am, but it'll serve; and there's an old shawl of Dulcie's somewhere about."

So Miranda changed her own plain skirt for the other, with its faded pattern of flowers; while Rosa, rummaging through a drawer, brought out an ancient flannel shawl, its original stuff so often mended with scraps of variously colored cloth as to resemble a piece of patchwork, along with a dingy kerchief which she tied over Miranda's hair so that it was altogether hidden away.

"You don't look much of a gypsy even now," Rosa said, frowning at her critically. "But here, we'll black your face a bit—it's lucky the fire was left to go out."

She took a handful of ashes from the stove, and with none too gentle a touch smeared their sooty powder over Miranda's face and down her neck. "That's better," she said, surveying her work. "A good thing you've dark eyes. Now, your hands." And she rubbed the ashes into their skin as well.

"I suppose you'll do," she said at last, turning Miranda to the glass. "There, my lady, what do you think of yourself?"

Miranda was a good deal startled by her own reflection.

For below the drab kerchief her eyes stared out from a mask of dull and sickly gray—far more like the face of some miserable beggar, or moping idiot, than a gypsy's. "I suppose we could pass you off as a half-wit," Rosa remarked callously, echoing Miranda's thoughts. "Though I don't believe your own mother'd recognize you now."

Miranda hardly knew whether to feel grateful or not. It was bad enough seeing herself made so ugly, but her heart sank even further at the thought of confronting Leo in this dismal disguise. In the end, however, she smiled bravely, and thanked Rosa for her help. The young woman only shrugged and, turning away, began to thrust into drawers and cupboards every loose object which might be unsettled by the caravan's motion.

Miranda could hear Dulcie's and Leo's voices outside, as they worked at harnessing the horse between the shafts; and presently Dulcie came in, saying that all was in order, the lanterns were lit, and Leo was staying on to drive their caravan that night.

Then she caught sight of Miranda's face, and could not help laughing—though she checked herself quickly, observing the girl's mournful expression. "I'm sorry, dear," she said. "It was only the surprise—why, I'd never have known you. Still, it seems you've got your wish—Rosa's turned you into a gypsy of sorts, hasn't she?"

But now, with an unexpected lurch, the caravan began to move across the field. Both sisters stumbled about, clutching at the last few articles that remained to be made secure; and as soon as everything was attended to, they prepared for bed, although for safety's sake Miranda got into her blankets wearing her gypsy clothes.

Then Dulcie blew out the candles, and darkness reigned; while the caravan slowly rumbled and clanked its way along the lane Miranda had traveled some hours before.

he procession of caravans did not retrace Miranda's steps, however, but followed the narrow lane farther into the depths of the countryside. Each rut and stone of their winding course lent itself to the discomforts of Miranda's hard bed on the floor, and she began to wonder whether she would ever fall asleep.

Indeed, she seemed to have remained conscious of every rattling mile; except that all at once she found the little windows grown bright, and the two women out of bed, Rosa tying on her kerchief before the mirror and Dulcie kindling a fire in the stove. The room was considerably colder than on the previous night, and now the boy awakened, too, shivering and complaining of hunger.

Having risen and folded up her blankets, Miranda stood about uncertainly, feeling very much in the way. But Dulcie spoke to her cheerfully. "We'll soon be warm now," she said, "and I expect it won't be long before we stop to eat. We've come a good distance, by the look of it."

Peering out one of the windows, Miranda discovered that the scene had changed from the woods and rolling hills of her own familiar landscape to level fields, spread out to a low horizon. "Wherever are we?" she asked in surprise.

"We're traveling east, towards the sea," said Dulcie. "Haven't you been this way before?"

"No, never," Miranda replied. "I've never been any-where near the seaside. Have we really come so far?"

"The sea's a long way yet," Dulcie answered. "We shan't get there for some days, the roundabout roads we take."

"And a fine place it'll be when we do," Rosa put in bitterly. "We stayed the winter on that coast once before, and once was enough. All heath and marsh, and the nearest town half a dozen miles off. I've no doubt Tom's making for the same spot again, thanks to some little noddy and her half-baked schemes."

Miranda could only look shamefaced. But just then the caravan drew up with a jolt, and there was a sound of men's voices outside. Dulcie, after a hurried glance through the window, turned back in alarm.

"It's two police constables," she whispered. "Perhaps they're only asking where we're bound, but we'd better be ready in any case. Quick, Miranda, go over by the stove, and if they come in, begin stirring up the fire. Make out that you don't understand what's said, even if you're spoken to—I'll answer for you."

Miranda did as she was told; and not long afterwards heavy feet mounted the steps, and there was a loud rap-ping at the door.

"Now then, let's have a look round," a man's voice declared, as Dulcie admitted one of the constables. "Four of you here, are there?" he questioned, casting a bold eye about the caravan. "I don't see beds for more than three."

"That's so, sir," Dulcie answered respectfully. "The boy shares his mother's; and that's my own daughter there by the stove. I'm afraid things are untidy, but we've only just got up."

The constable merely grunted in reply and moved about looking beneath the bunks, while Miranda, lifting the stove lid, began to stir the fire with a poker.

"Turn this way a moment, my girl," ordered the constable, stepping nearer to Miranda; but she had the good sense not to respond. "Didn't you hear me, then?" he asked her sharply.

"You'll have to excuse my daughter, sir, she's weak in the head," Dulcie explained, taking the poker away from Miranda, "and she will meddle with the fire. Burnt herself more than once, she has—but there, the poor thing knows no better. Come away now, dear." She put her arm about Miranda's shoulders and sat her down on the bed, while Miranda, staring vacantly, her mouth agape, attempted to look as witless as possible.

"What's happened to her face?" the constable inquired, vaguely suspicious, bending down to peer at Miranda's cheek.

"Ah, sir, the poor soul's always tumbling down, or knocking into something. She's harmless to others unless they tease her, but she's a danger to herself and that's a fact."

The constable straightened up with a visible shudder. "Well, see you look after her better," he said uneasily, moving towards the door. "It doesn't do to let such creatures roam about."

"Yes, sir, thank you, sir," Dulcie replied with a curtsy, as he took his leave.

"No sign of her there," they heard him say to his companion, who had also come back empty-handed. "Like as not she's run off with some man—that's most often the way of it." And both of them chuckled knowingly. "Move along, then," he called out to the drivers, "and don't let us hear of you giving any trouble—none of your gypsy tricks, mind."

After the caravans were safely on their way again, the sisters looked at one another and went off into such peals of laughter that Miranda could not avoid smiling as well, although she suspected her own appearance to be the cause of it.

But Dulcie, still laughing, laid a hand on her arm. "Don't take offense, dear," she gasped. "It's not just on your account. Didn't you see his face? I believe you gave him a nasty turn!"

Rosa herself grinned at Miranda, in a better humor than before. "I must say you acted a proper simpleton," she acknowledged. "Though of course those ashes made all the difference."

"Of course they did," agreed Miranda readily, heartened by this first sign of thaw on Rosa's part. "Just think, he'd have taken me away by now, if it hadn't been for the two of you."

"Well, it wasn't only for your sake," Rosa reminded her. "We'd our own skins to save, too. But there, it's no good keeping on about it, and I'll give you credit for some sense, after all."

"Now, that's better," said Dulcie. "Come along, Miranda, and help me to make up the beds. We'll surely be stopping in a little while."

They had traveled no more than a mile or so farther before the horses were reined in and the caravans drawn up at the side of the road. Miranda followed Dulcie outside, to find herself in the midst of a broad plain, with not a house in sight, and only a few willows and poplars fringing the windswept meadows. The large, sturdy horses were soon unharnessed and tethered in an adjacent field, where they fell to cropping the grass; while the gypsies set about fetching water from a nearby stream and collecting such sticks as they could find to make a fire.

At first Miranda looked about apprehensively for Leo; but he had gone away to confer with Tom, and afterwards she only caught a distant glimpse of him, walking along with the dog. Once a fire was kindled, however, and some of the gypsies had gathered to await the boiling of an iron pot set above its flames, Miranda spied Leo a little way off, busy with something on the ground; and before long he came over to them, bearing the skinned and gutted carcass of a rabbit, which was cut up directly, and the pieces thrown into the pot.

"You may thank your stars that dog's a good rabbiter," observed Rosa, at Miranda's side. "Otherwise, we'd have had nothing for breakfast but potatoes. Or perhaps they don't fancy rabbit at your house?" She favored Miranda with a mocking smile.

"I've never eaten it," Miranda confessed. "But I'm so

hungry this morning I'm sure I could fancy anything."
And when at last the rabbit and potatoes were cooked up
together, Miranda thought she had never tasted anything
so good—though her portion of rabbit was hardly more
than a mouthful, and the potatoes were few enough themselves.

After their meal, Rosa took Jemmy off to pick some
of the mushrooms scattered about the fields, while those
who had been driving all night retired to their caravans
to rest for an hour or two. But several women and children stayed by the fire, and Dulcie led Miranda round to
introduce her, the other gypsies having so far kept their
distance, only casting inquisitive glances at her from time
to time.

She had, in fact, found no difficulty in avoiding Tom,
of whom she was still much in awe. He had remained at
the other side of the fire while they were eating, along
with Leo and two women Miranda had not seen before,
and afterwards went away to his own caravan without a
look in her direction. But now Dulcie drew her over to
those women who had sat beside him.

"It's high time you met Miranda," she said to them.
"Miranda, here's Tom's wife, Nan, and her mother,
Bella. I'm glad to see you out today, Nan—you're feeling
better, then?"

"Oh, I'm right enough this morning," Nan replied
placidly; although in truth she looked far from well, her
face, clearly handsome once, grown hollow-cheeked, and
her skin unhealthily sallow. "So you're the one the fuss

(35)

was about," she said to Miranda with a smile. "And it seems you're to stop with us for a bit, at least—though I'm afraid Tom still doesn't like it."

"Well, Dulcie, you've turned her into a queer sort of gypsy, I must say," put in Bella, an old woman with eyes that shone dark and brilliant in her wrinkled face.

"That's Rosa's work," Dulcie told her. "She's overdone it, perhaps."

"I don't wonder she took in the constables," said Bella, laughing. "Though it's a shame to spoil a pretty face—isn't it, my dear?" she asked, turning to Miranda.

"I don't really mind it," Miranda answered half-heartedly. "Only I wish I could look more like the rest of you."

"Come now, Dulcie," said Bella, "can't we serve her better than this? What about those walnuts we gathered a while ago? They'd give a good color, and it wouldn't come off so easily. And we might find her some earrings as well."

"That would look better," Dulcie agreed. "What do you say, Miranda?"

"Yes, please," Miranda replied eagerly. "If you think Rosa wouldn't mind."

"Here then, Dulcie," said the old woman, "fetch us some water, and a couple of heavy stones. I'll bring the walnuts, and I know I've an old pair of earrings put away. Ah, but wait a moment—you've no holes to your ears, have you, my dear? What about that? Will you have some made? It's easy enough, and we'll do it just now, if you like."

Miranda looked at Dulcie. "Does it hurt much?" she asked doubtfully.

"Nothing to speak of, and it's soon over," Dulcie assured her. "But of course it's for you to decide."

"Well, if I'm to be a gypsy, I expect I'd better," Miranda replied, with a gallant attempt at a smile.

"That's the spirit," Bella commended her. "Then I'll bring a needle as well. You go along with Dulcie to the stream, and clean your face for a start. We'll have you set to rights in no time at all."

etermined to show no fear, Miranda walked with Dulcie to the shallow stream, where she bathed her hands and face; her cheek still ached, but the swelling was less, and the cold water felt fresh and soothing to her skin. Dulcie, having filled a pail, prised out two good-sized stones from the stream bed, and they carried these back to the fire, where Nan and the others waited.

A small potful of water was set over the coals; and soon Bella returned with a knobbly sack containing a quantity of green-husked walnuts, which Dulcie pounded one by one between the stones, dropping their crushed fragments into the water. When the pot had boiled, the brew was put aside to steep and cool; while Bella, sitting down with Miranda, made ready to pierce her left earlobe.

Just at that moment, however, Miranda caught sight of Leo walking from the caravans in their direction. She drew back, startled, and Bella stayed her hand.

"Nay, Leo, be off with you!" she called to him, laughing. "Don't come this way till we've finished—though later there'll be a pretty enough sight to behold." And the old woman gave Miranda a wink that set her blushing.

Leo had turned back at once, without a word. But now, when Miranda felt the needle's sharp stab, she clenched her fists, and thought only of how she soon might face him again without shame.

The old woman worked quickly, with steady hands; and after she had run the needle through Miranda's other lobe, and stopped the bleeding, she drew from her pocket a pair of small gold hoops, worn with age, but softly gleaming still.

"These were mine, when I was a girl," she said quietly, holding out the earrings on her palm. "I hope you'll show yourself worthy of them, my dear, and never betray them—for they're gypsy gold, given in trust, and not to be treated lightly." She gazed into Miranda's eyes with an expression the girl could not fathom; nor could she think how to answer this solemn charge.

But then, without further ado, Bella fixed the rings in Miranda's ears. Dulcie, smiling, said that they looked very well; while Nan and the other women who sat watching murmured their own approval.

Next Bella turned to the brew of walnuts; and dipping in her fingers, she smoothed the murky liquid over Miranda's face and neck and hands, again and again, letting it dry between anointments. At first, as Miranda surveyed the backs of her hands, they only looked a dullish yellow. But as the slow daubing continued, they deepened to a darker gold, and thence to a warm brown; until at length every visible portion of her skin was stained the same rich color.

"There, that's far better," said the old woman, setting the pot aside. "Now we'll find a bottle to hold what's left, so you can put on more whenever it's needed; and you'll keep as brown as any of us, my dear."

"Oh, thank you, Bella!" Miranda cried in delight. "It's so much nicer than the other. And thank you for the earrings, too. You've been so kind to me, just like Dulcie."

"That's a good girl," said Dulcie, with as much pride as if Miranda had been her own daughter. "But you'd better go straightaway and show yourself to Rosa, as I see they're coming back. And let's hope she's filled her basket, so you'll find her in a good temper."

Miranda walked off obediently to meet her. But Rosa, catching sight of Miranda's face, dropped Jemmy's hand and stared at her open-mouthed.

Miranda hastened forward, and spoke before the other could say anything. "I hope you don't mind, Rosa," she began anxiously. "You'd done it all so cleverly before, and I would have stayed just as I was—only Bella thought of the walnuts, and she'd some earrings to spare. And I did so want to look a proper gypsy."

Rosa had set down her basket—well filled with mushrooms, as it happened; and as she listened to Miranda, her face took on an amused smile. "Well, I can't say I blame you," she admitted. "But don't go thinking you'll be a gypsy all at once," she added quickly. "You've got to prove yourself, and Tom won't be taken in by your looks, however much they've changed."

"I know it, Rosa," Miranda said humbly. "And I'll do my best; only don't be angry with me any longer."

"Come now, my girl, I'm not such a bear as you might think," Rosa replied. "Though I'm more careful than Dulcie; she's always had a soft heart for strays, and besides, there's her own daughter who died—I don't expect she's told you about that. It happened in the fire when both of us lost our husbands, and Dulcie's never entirely got over it. But here, bring that basket along. There's mushrooms enough for everybody, I daresay."

Taking Jemmy's hand again, Rosa strode on without another word; and Miranda, picking up the basket, followed with a lighter heart than she had known in many a day.

By now the gypsies who had retired earlier were returning to the fire. While the mushrooms grilled on skewers over its flames, Dulcie presented Miranda to those of the company she had not met before; and although she was treated to some joking on the subject of her new disguise, it pleased Miranda to think that she now looked much like these gypsies herself—as, indeed, their skin was not so very different in color from hers, and women and children alike, and even some of the men, wore hoops of gold in their ears.

Once the mushrooms were eaten, two or three women went off gathering additional sticks to take along for their stoves, and Miranda accompanied Dulcie on the same errand. Sighting, two fields away, what looked to be a small coppice, they made for that; and found beneath its isolated cluster of trees a good many fallen twigs and branches, which they collected in two rough piles, breaking the branches to more manageable lengths. As they were attempting, with difficulty, to gather these up in their arms, they heard a whistle, and Leo appeared, walking towards them.

"You've come at the right moment, Leo," called Dulcie.

"We've found as much as we can carry, and more. Here, Miranda, give Leo some of yours, and I'll do the same."

"They're in rather a tangle," said Miranda, trying to loosen a portion of her sticks from the rest—which only resulted in most of them falling to the ground. "Oh dear," she apologized, bending awkwardly to retrieve them, "they will catch at one another!"

But glancing up in chagrin, she saw that Leo waited calmly, without the slightest impatience. "Let me do it, then," he said at last, stooping down beside her; and he set about making two heaps of the unwieldy bundle.

Miranda stood by, watching his lean brown hands as he worked, thinking how neat and adept they looked. And remembering, by contrast, that soft, damp handshake of her suitor's, she was overcome by an exultant sense of her deliverance.

How lucky she was to have fallen in with such folk as Dulcie, and Bella, and Leo! Indeed, she could scarcely summon up a pang of remorse at abandoning her parents; though it occurred to her now that if only they had found her a suitor more like Leo, she would certainly not have run away from home. On the other hand, she felt sure that among their acquaintances there was nobody in the least like him; and looking down again at his black curly head and thin strong shoulders, she wondered whether there was any young man as nice as Leo in all the world.

Still, she could find no word or gesture to express what she felt just then, except to thank him with a smile as he stood up and lifted her share of sticks into her arms. Leo smiled in return; and made suddenly bold, she said to him, "How is it some of the other men wear earrings, and yet you don't yourself?" Though the next moment, taken aback by the impudent sound of her words, she wished she had held her tongue.

But Leo simply replied, "There's some do, and some don't—I never fancied them for myself. Too much like a bull with a ring in its nose, perhaps. Yours suit you well enough, though," he added hastily; and his eyes met Miranda's with a look of admiration that sent the blood rushing to her face.

"I'm glad you think so," she murmured, not daring to say anything further, since Dulcie had by now divided up her own sticks and stood waiting for Leo to collect his portion. She had not seemed to take much heed of their conversation; but Miranda wondered, as they walked back towards the caravans, whether Dulcie would have minded if she had known everything that Miranda felt about her son.

While she shrank from the thought of displeasing Dulcie, she could not resist hoping that there was more to Leo's friendliness than mere good nature—and on the heels of these speculations, it came into her head that she might ask Dulcie to tell her fortune, after all.

She was, however, given no opportunity to mention it just then, as they discovered the rest of the party prepared to move off. Rosa, to whom the driving had fallen this time, sat mounted at the front of the caravan, holding the reins very capably, and before long the procession had set forth again.

The afternoon wore on, the stove lent its warmth to their little room, and Miranda, watching Dulcie quietly mending a pair of stockings, found herself so contented that she hardly minded the hunger that plagued her, or the twinges she felt if she touched her ears. From time to time she stealthily admired the darkened skin of her hands, and once or twice stole a glance in the mirror at her reflection—which seemed to belong to quite a different person, as though she had changed in more than just appearance, and assumed some other character along with her gypsy disguise.

But at length growing restless, and stirred by these strange impressions, she ventured to ask the question still at the back of her mind. "Dulcie, do you suppose I might have my fortune told?"

Dulcie smiled. "I wondered if you'd be bringing that up," she said. "It was fortunes we first talked about in the market, wasn't it?"

"Well, I'd nearly forgotten, with so much else to think about," replied Miranda, "and I'd the notion then of learning to tell fortunes myself." She felt more than a little sheepish, for it seemed a pitifully green and ignorant girl who had stood by the gypsies' barrow only the day before. "Still, I would like to hear my own fortune," she went on, "though I've no money, except that coin I've given Jemmy."

"Bless you," laughed Dulcie, "we'd never ask you to

cross our palms with silver now! Besides, we've one kind of fortune-telling for other folk, and a different sort for ourselves—and I think you'd better have ours, since you've already become so much of a gypsy."

"Then will you tell mine, Dulcie, please?" Miranda asked.

"Nay, not I, dear," Dulcie answered her, "though I can lay out the ordinary cards well enough, or read off any-one's palm in the usual way. But Bella's the one you must go to. She's got a pack of the old gypsy cards, and she sees things there the rest of us couldn't, even if we tried. She has the true gift for it, you know—the sight, as it's called—that's not found so often nowadays as it used to be. Yes, I believe Bella would read your cards if you asked her," she continued thoughtfully. "She's read all ours—though my fortune wasn't so happy, and often I've wished I hadn't known about the sorrows to come."

Miranda put out her hand and touched the other's gently. "I know, Dulcie," she said. "Rosa told me today, about your daughter."

"Ah, did she," said Dulcie; and seemed to ponder before she spoke again. "But she couldn't have told you something else Bella saw in my cards, something I've kept to myself all these years. For she said I'd lose one daugh-ter, but find another to take her place—'a dark girl lost, and a fair one found,' she told me. Isn't that odd, now?" She looked at Miranda with a singular expression.

"Even when you first spoke to us at the market, I felt there was a purpose behind it," she said softly, "and it nearly broke my heart to turn you away. But I knew that if it was meant to be, you'd come to us somehow—and so you did, in spite of everything."

"Why, Dulcie, do you really think I'm the one that was meant?" Miranda asked, amazed. "If it's true, it's the strangest thing I ever heard. Though I'd like to be your other daughter," she added earnestly. "You've already been kinder to me than my own mother was."

"Nay, you mustn't speak ill of your mother," said Dulcie gravely. "Whatever mistakes she's made, you're bound to her by flesh and blood, and I've no doubt you'll go home one day and make things right between you. Still, if Tom lets you stay, I'll gladly act as your second mother for a time. You needn't say anything about it to the rest, though I believe Bella's seen it, and that's one reason she's been so helpful; and Nan may know something about it, too."

"I'll keep it between us, of course," Miranda promised, though she could not help wondering all the more about Leo, and whether Dulcie's fortune might not have some bearing on his own. But she dared not speak of him even now; and soon after that they made ready for bed, as Jemmy had long ago fallen asleep, Miranda's coin once more held tight in his hand.

But tonight, when the candles were extinguished, the caravan's rattle and jolt, rather than disturbing Miranda, soothed her; and though she was wearing an old night-dress of Dulcie's, as threadbare as it was plain, she slept on the hard floor as peacefully as she might have in fine frilled muslin, snug in her bed at home.

hen Miranda awoke the next morning, the caravans had drawn to a halt. Rosa soon came in with the news that they were stopping at a farm and must look sharp, as there was a day's work to be had, and the farmer's wife might buy a hamper if it suited her.

So Dulcie and Rosa wheeled the barrow away; while Miranda, having paused briefly to dab her hands and face afresh with walnut brew, led Jemmy after them to the low, ramshackle farmhouse. She found Dulcie standing at its back doorway with the farmer's wife, who was examining the contents of the barrow with a critical eye, and who now looked up sharply at Miranda.

"I hope there's no more to come," she said. "I doubt we've food enough to give the lot of you much of a supper. But if your men get that wood split, and the cow-shed's cleaned out properly, I'll find some bread and cheese, and see if there's apples to spare. Yes, and I expect it'll take your women all day to get through the washing, I'm that behind," she went on in a complaining voice, "what with my husband laid up, and only myself and my daughter to see to every blessed thing. Come along, then, I'll have that larger hamper—at least it looks better made than the rubbish those last gypsies came selling. Will you want the money, or put it towards something more for your suppers?"

"Thank you, ma'am, we'll have the money, if you

please," replied Dulcie. "And if you've another sixpence or two, perhaps you and your daughter would like your fortunes told."

"Fortunes, indeed!" the woman retorted. "We've neither time nor money to waste on such nonsense. You'd better get along to the washhouse with the others, and not come pestering honest folk with your gypsy lies."

Dulcie only curtsied in reply, and the farmer's wife turned back into the house with her purchase; although before the door was shut, Miranda caught a glimpse of her daughter peering out at them wistfully, as if she would not have minded having her own fortune told.

Left in charge of Jemmy for the day, Miranda pushed the barrow home again; and afterwards, holding the boy's hand, she strolled along the line of caravans, pausing now and then to admire the gaily carved fretwork about their eaves, and their stout wheels, painted a brilliant red, if at present badly scratched and weathered.

She had it in mind to wander farther down the lane, for want of any better diversion; but when they reached the foremost of the caravans and stopped to pay their respects to the dog Bruno, lying beneath it on his chain, Bella put her head out the door.

"Good morning to you, Miranda," she said. "Will you come inside? It's chilly damp weather, isn't it?"

Miranda readily mounted the steps with Jemmy in tow, and entered to find herself in another small room like Dulcie's, though this one appeared even more crowded, with an additional bunk in place of a dresser, and a greater profusion of articles hung about the walls. On one of the bunks, Nan, Tom's wife, lay beneath several blankets; she was awake, but spoke only a brief word of greeting, and afterwards shut her eyes, while Bella drew the covers closer about her.

"We'll try not to disturb you, dear," she said. "But it'll do you good to have a bit of company, even if you only lie quiet.

"Poor thing," she said to Miranda in a low voice, "she oughtn't to have stopped out so long yesterday. She's not been well, you know, since a summer ago, when we stayed in the south. She came down with a fever there that's never left her, in spite of all the remedies we've tried; and some days she's hot and cold by turns, with her head aching so she can't bear to stir. But just you and Jemmy sit down and I'll make us a pot of tea—you've had no breakfast, I suppose?"

"No," Miranda admitted, "though the farmer's wife said there'd be bread and cheese, and apples; only I think we won't be given them until the day's over."

"That's how it is," sighed Bella, taking a steaming kettle from the stove. "They don't trust us not to eat and be off before the work's properly finished. Though I'm sorry to say there's others might behave so—even Tom's brother was something of a rascal. That's why Tom fell out with him, and we've gone our own ways ever since. And a hard road it's been at times, with Nan so ill, not to mention the fire—you've heard about that, perhaps?"

"Only a little," Miranda replied. "I know Dulcie's and

Rosa's husbands died—and Dulcie's daughter, too." She glanced at the old woman hesitantly, thinking of her conversation with Dulcie the day before.

But Bella, busy over the tea leaves, did not look up. "Yes, it was an awful time," she said. "More than three years ago, it is now. We'd gone to some fair, and they came back early, Rosa's husband, and Dulcie's, and her daughter, who was feeling poorly. The men had brought home the money we'd earned at the fair, so as to put it away safe—for there's many who'd rob a gypsy and think they'd done no wrong.

"At all events," she went on, in the meantime pouring out for Miranda a mugful of bitter, fragrant tea, which she sipped with grateful relish, "they were waiting in one of the caravans for the rest to come home. Only something must have gone amiss with the stove, and they were overcome before they knew what was happening— because by the time the others got there, the caravan was up in flames, with the three of them still inside. Oh, it was a terrible business! I thought Dulcie would never be herself again, she grieved so. And the worst of it was that I'd read it in her cards—widowhood, and a daughter lost, all of it, years before—so she'd known it was to come, even though she tried to think it was meant some other way."

"Oh, poor Dulcie," mourned Miranda, struck more than ever by the pity of it. "And poor Rosa, too."

"Rosa took it better, somehow," said Bella, "though I think she's grown a bit hard since. Still, she didn't lose a child. Jemmy was just a baby at the time, and she was kept occupied looking after him. Of course, Leo's been a comfort to Dulcie; and there were other things I'd seen in her cards that gave her the heart to go on." Now she looked at Miranda keenly.

"Oh, Bella, she told me about it," Miranda exclaimed. "A daughter lost, but another one found—it's so strange, isn't it? I mean, how you could see it, years ago, that I'd come to her. At least, I do hope I'm the one that was meant," she ended anxiously.

"If she's told you, then it's certain you're the one," Bella assured her. "And Nan and I both thought of it the very night you came, didn't we, dear?" she said to her daughter, who opened her eyes again and gave Miranda a faint smile.

"We did," she replied. "And I must say we've had a time of it since, trying to persuade Tom to keep you."

"Aye, he's not at all sure he's done the right thing," said Bella. "But with the cards in your favor, I shouldn't be surprised if he saw his way to it in the end."

"Bella," Miranda inquired timidly, "I wanted to ask you—would you tell my own fortune? Dulcie said you were the only one who knew the true way of it."

"Ah, I wonder now," Bella said, looking at Miranda with her head on one side. "Have you some reason in particular for wanting to know about the future? Your present life's eventful enough, I'd have said."

"Just to know if Tom will let me stay, or whether I'll ever go home again," Miranda answered uneasily, avoiding the old woman's eye. "And if I'll be married someday, that sort of thing."

"Yes, I thought it might be that last," said Bella. "Of course, it's only to be expected, at your age. And yet I wonder whether you haven't thought more on that subject since you came to us."

"I'm afraid to say so, Bella," Miranda faltered, her eyes averted still. "I'm afraid Dulcie might not like it. Because I'm not a real gypsy, am I, even though you've made me look like one? And perhaps it's not right that I should feel as I do about—about one of you."

"I believe I can set your mind at rest on that score, at least," Bella said gently. "For if Dulcie's already taken to thinking of you as a daughter, I don't expect she'd mind you being fond of her son. But as to your own feelings, and what comes of them, that's for time and the cards to say. If they bear you out, then it's all one whether you've gypsy blood in your veins or not."

"Oh, thank you, Bella," Miranda said fervently, looking into the old woman's face at last. "That helps me to feel much easier. And will you read the cards for me, please?"

"Very well, my dear, if you've your heart set on it," Bella consented. "Though we'll wait till we've made camp again, and the proper moment comes along. Just put it out of your mind for the time being; but I've a sense things will come right for you, if you're patient."

Then Miranda set down her empty cup, and took Jemmy away. But though she tried hard through the rest of that day not to think about all the old woman had said, she could not help wondering what her cards might reveal, and whether some sign concerning Leo lay hidden among them even now.

That evening, when the work was done, the gypsies, given their food to take home, withdrew into their caravans. A chill rain had begun to fall, but Dulcie lit the stove again and soon the room grew comfortably warm.

Her hunger stayed at last, Miranda was feeling rather drowsy, when there came a hesitant tap at the door. Dulcie rose to open it; and there, with a shawl thrown over her head against the rain, stood the girl Miranda had seen at the farmhouse that morning, her face wan and a little frightened.

"If you please," she said, glancing behind her as if she might have been followed, "I want my fortune told."

"Come in, then, miss," Dulcie said, drawing the girl inside and shutting the door again. "What a nasty wet night it is, to be sure. Here, give me your shawl."

"I can't stop long," said the girl, looking about her nervously. "Mother didn't want me to come, but I waited my chance and slipped out."

"There, of course," said Dulcie, motioning her to sit down on one of the beds. "Daughters do seem to visit us more often than their mothers. There's more in store for them, isn't there?"

The girl smiled weakly, her eyes still darting about the caravan in a mixture of curiosity and apprehension.

"Have you brought some money with you, miss?" asked Rosa, in less obliging tones than Dulcie's.

"I'd only a threepenny bit of my own—I hope it's enough," replied the girl, taking a coin from her pocket.

"That'll do very well," Dulcie asserted, with a stern look at Rosa. "I'll just fetch out the cards. Or perhaps you'd like me to read your palm instead?"

"I don't mind," the girl answered. "I suppose I'd better have whichever one's quicker. Mother'll be that vexed if she finds me gone."

"Come along, then, give me your hand," said Dulcie kindly, sitting down beside her. "Ah, see there: you've a long life before you, to start with, and good health, from the look of it. But now, what's this? Two marriages! The first short, the second one long, but both of them happy; and two, three, four children! I can't make out if they're all of the same marriage, but they're fine healthy children, in any event. Though there's a setback, too. It seems you'll be poor for a time; but you'll weather it out, and live on to a ripe old age, as I said before. You've a good strong hand, my dear; there's many could wish for one like it."

"Does it really show I'm to have two husbands?" the girl asked eagerly, her pinched face grown for the moment quite pretty.

"There they are, plain as plain," Dulcie replied, pointing out a couple of small creases. "And the first before very long, I'd say."

"Oh, but if I know the first's to die," the girl said, her face clouding, "won't I always be thinking of it, and fretting over it?"

"It's true, you may find that hard," Dulcie agreed

sympathetically. "But then you've always the thought of the second one to comfort you." And she cast a brief smile towards Miranda.

"All the same, I think I'd rather not have known," the girl said in a peevish voice, standing up again. "Perhaps Mother was right, and it's only gypsy nonsense."

"Isn't that the way of it," Rosa exclaimed from where she stood watching with folded arms. "Folk think they want to hear the future, but then when it's not everything they'd hoped, they lay the blame at our door."

"Nay, Rosa, I'm sure this young lady has more sense," Dulcie said calmly. "Just you be glad of the good things I've told you, my dear, and don't brood over the rest. Each will come to you in its own way, and you've only to be ready to make the best of them."

"I don't know," said the girl, frowning at her palm distrustfully. "It's hard to believe you could see so much in a few little lines." Then, with a shrug, she put on her shawl and went away.

After she was gone, Rosa sat down again, looking thoroughly disgusted. "I wonder you kept your temper, Dulcie," she said, "with the little chit grumbling so— and only giving you threepence, at that."

"Never mind, Rosa," Dulcie sighed. "At least the poor thing's got something to think about now. I expect her life's hard enough otherwise."

"But could you really see all those things?" Miranda asked. "I thought you'd said you weren't much at telling fortunes—but it sounded as if you knew everything about her, as soon as you looked at her hand."

"Oh well," said Dulcie, faintly embarrassed, "there's enough in anybody's hand to make a tale of. Some lines are perfectly clear, and there's no art to reading them off in the ordinary way. But if I had the real gift, like Bella, I'd be able to see far more."

"I asked Bella today if she'd tell my fortune," Miranda admitted, "and she said she would, when we're settled again."

"Well, I hope you've learned a lesson tonight," Rosa cautioned her, "so you won't go about complaining if you don't like what you hear."

"I'm sure I won't," Miranda replied in some indignation.

"Now then, don't mind Rosa," Dulcie told her. "She's just out of temper from driving last night, and standing most of today with her hands in soapy water."

Rosa laughed shortly. "Those petticoats were a ragged lot, weren't they, Dulcie?" she observed. "It seems that girl's not been taught much about mending—a fine wife she'll make, indeed."

"I tried to learn sewing once," Miranda confessed. "But I wasn't any good at it. My mother used to say my fingers were all thumbs."

"Well, you'd better try again, if you're to stop with us," said Rosa with a grin. "You'll have no new clothes for a long while, and those old ones won't last unless you look after them."

"Oh dear, I suppose I must," said Miranda, troubled. "But I've always been so stupid about such things. I wasn't much use at cookery, either."

"You'll do better when there's need for it," Rosa returned lightly. "And we'll have you making baskets, too, before you know it."

"Baskets!" Miranda exclaimed. "Oh no, I don't believe I could ever learn anything like that."

Dulcie smiled. "Don't trouble yourself over it," she said. "We'll show you the way, never fear. There now, we've talked too late as it is, and we'll be off early in the morning."

But afterwards Miranda turned restlessly in her blankets, as if the caravan had been jolting along instead of standing quiet at the side of the road; and all night it seemed that her mind was trying to weave impossible patterns out of crooked twigs, which caught at one another and refused to be untangled in spite of her every effort.

ext day the rain fell harder than ever, and gusty winds shook the caravan, piercing its chinks with dismal drafts. Although it was Dulcie's turn to drive that morning, Leo insisted on taking her place, to which, after some protest, she agreed. The lanes were slippery with mud, and their progress was slow. Rosa remained in a petulant humor, grumbling over the cold and the damp—the more so when their last sticks were consumed and the stove went out altogether.

Miranda did her best to amuse Jemmy by showing him how to play games on his fingers, church-and-steeple, and the two blackbirds, and the fishes. But the child soon tired of these, and Miranda could think of no others. In the end they all fell silent, except for Jemmy, who chattered and whined by turns, and drummed the heels of his boots against the bunk frame until Rosa lost her temper and smacked him: upon which he wailed, and afterwards sniffed so unceasingly that Miranda could almost have smacked him herself.

At noon they ate what was left of the bread and cheese, and the few remaining apples. Faced with the likelihood of nothing else to eat that day, Miranda felt even more depressed. But Dulcie brought out some mending, which distracted Rosa a little, and the two of them stitched in comparative peace for a time.

Presently, however, Rosa looked up from her work at Miranda, who was sitting idle beside the boy, now mercifully asleep. "If you've nothing else to do, my girl," she said tartly, "perhaps you'd give us a hand with some of this mending."

Miranda stared at her in dismay. "Oh, I don't think I'd better," she replied. "You don't know what a botch I'd make of it—you'd be sorry I tried."

"Nonsense," returned Rosa. "If you haven't learned to sew before, it's high time you did now. Besides, any numbskull can set on a patch. I'll even pin it in place, so you've only to stitch round the edges."

Looking to Dulcie for help, Miranda merely received an encouraging smile. So she accepted the garment Rosa handed her—a shirt of Jemmy's, out at one elbow—and, with a hopeless shrug, set to work as best she could.

The long thread tangled at the first stitch, and by the time Miranda had unraveled that knot, another had formed, so that she was obliged to break off her cotton and begin again. She felt Rosa's eyes upon her, and flushed; but working on doggedly, if slowly, and often pricking her fingers, she sewed round the patch in rather a haphazard fashion.

"Here, let's see how you've managed," Rosa said, putting aside her own work and coming over to her. "Bless us, child, is that the best you can do? Why, those stitches wouldn't hold fast a day."

"I told you I couldn't do it properly," cried Miranda, stung to anger, throwing the shirt down on the bed. "I believe you expected it, too, and only wanted to shame me. It's not fair!"

Now Rosa herself looked ashamed. "There, Miranda,

Blairsville High School Library

don't take on so," she said, with a guilty glance at her sister. "I suppose you're right, and it was mainly my own vexation, seeing you sit there watching and woolgathering. It does seem odd, though, not knowing how to do something that easy—why, I was taught to darn stockings when I was half your age."

"Yes, but Mother had more patience than you do, Rosa," put in Dulcie, "and I'm sure I couldn't work properly either, with someone glowering at me the whole time."

Miranda gave Dulcie a grateful smile, and picked up the shirt again. "Shall I take it out and begin over?" she asked repentantly.

"Nay, never mind," said Rosa with a sigh. "I'll see to it later on. Though I hope it won't be like this over the baskets. You may not be cut out for such work, but you've got to make some effort if you're to learn anything."

"That's what my mother used to say," Miranda told her ruefully. "Only she gave it up in the end; and then they decided to marry me off to a rich husband, so I shouldn't have to do a thing for myself."

"Well, you'd better turn over a new leaf now," said Rosa sardonically, "for there's never a gypsy wife who's waited on hand and foot, that's certain."

Miranda blushed, unable to meet either Rosa's or Dulcie's eyes. But at that moment, with a jerk and a shudder, the caravan came to a halt; and Dulcie, stepping outside briefly, came back to say that they were stopping for the night.

After another half hour or so, the sisters put away their

mending and began to prepare for bed. Miranda unfolded her blankets, but before she had laid them out, there came a knock, and Leo, holding a lantern, appeared at the door. "Tom wants to see Miranda," he said. "I'm to take her back with me."

Miranda's heart sank. Whatever could Tom want with her at this time of night? Indeed, she could think of no reason for her summons unless he had made up his mind to send her away. Hastily she put on her shawl; and, as an afterthought, bent down to unfasten the coin from Jemmy's fingers where he lay asleep. Then, hardly daring to look at Leo, she followed him out into the rain.

The night was pitch-black beyond the lantern's dim illumination, and Miranda was thankful when Leo caught hold of her hand to draw her along through the mire and the dark. His own hand felt warm, and she clung to it tightly, barely able to see where she trod, yet so glad of that handclasp that she would have followed wherever it led.

Leo said not a word, and Miranda had not the courage to question him. But they soon made their way past the other caravans, and entered his own. Looking about her timidly, Miranda saw that Tom stood next to the stove, his face set and austere; but although she found Nan sitting up in bed, with Bella seated beside her, she could not tell from either's expression whether to feel hopeful or afraid.

At first Tom only gazed at her in silence. Then, after a long moment, he moved towards Miranda and put out a hand to her face. She nearly flinched, reminded of the blow he had dealt her before. But Tom merely touched her cheek, and said in a gruff voice, "I see that's mending right enough."

"Yes," Miranda replied faintly. "It wasn't so bad, really."

"Not that it'd show so much now," Tom said with unremitting gravity. "You've changed color since last we met."

"Yes," Miranda repeated, still unable to make out his purpose.

"You'll be wondering why I sent for you," he began, appearing almost as uneasy as she. "Well, I may as well tell you that I'd vowed to leave you behind after the very first day, to make your way home as best you could. Yes, and I'd have done so, if it hadn't been for these two"— he nodded towards Nan and Bella—"forever at me to keep you a bit longer.

"And even today," he continued, "as I sat there driving through the rain and the mud, thinking how this journey was all your fault, I said to myself that it wasn't too late. I could turn you out yet, and we'd go on to some likelier place for the winter, instead of hiding away in the loneliest spot I could think of. But when I came in tonight, and said I'd determined to have done with you at last, there was such a rumpus as never I heard!" He grimaced, albeit with the ghost of a grin. "You must have a touch of gypsy about you at that, the way you've got round these women till they're ready to do battle for you—even my poor old Nan."

Although Miranda kept silent, her pulse quickened with new hope.

"So hear me now," Tom pursued, looking at her hard. "We'll come to the sea the day after tomorrow, and we won't be moving on again all winter, unless something further goes awry. And though I've agreed, against my better judgment, to let you stop with us—nay, don't speak a word until I've done—I want it understood that if there's the least trouble on your account you'll be sent packing, and no mistake. Or if ever I hear you've been grumbling, or shirking your duties, it'll be the same—do you see?"

"Yes, Tom," replied Miranda meekly; but her eyes shone. "I'll do my best, I promise. And oh, thank you, Tom!"

"Nay, don't thank me," Tom said, with a grudging smile. "Thank these blessed women, who've worn me out with their talk. Though it seems you've behaved yourself well enough so far. Just see you go on as you've begun, so I'll not be sorry I gave way."

Miranda now put her hand in her pocket and brought out the gold sovereign. "I've meant you to have this," she said, "for the bother I've been, and to help pay for my keep. I offered it to Dulcie, but she wouldn't take it; so I hoped you might—" She broke off in confusion, as Tom had begun to frown again.

"Put your gold away, my girl," he said sternly. "You may think to buy favor of us, but there's none here will take anybody's money without its being properly earned. We've done naught but treat you as one of us, and you're mistaken if you're thinking to pay for that."

"Nay, Tom, she meant well," put in Bella. "But I tell

you what, my dear. If you like, I'll look after the coin till you've need of it again. Perhaps there's some other use awaiting it, and in the meantime it'll be safe enough with me."

"Yes, I suppose that would be best," Miranda agreed. "Though Jemmy will be sorry to give it up, I'm afraid."

"Ah, that's true," said Bella thoughtfully. "Perhaps it might be even better if he was the one to have charge of it."

"But won't he be likely to lose it?" Miranda asked in some surprise.

"Then it'll be a matter for fate to decide," replied Bella with a curious smile. "Gold's a funny thing, you know, and sometimes it's best left to its own devices."

"Let the boy have it, then," Tom chafed, though he frowned no longer, "and we'll say no more on the subject. Here now, missy, it's time you were off to your bed, and us to ours."

"Yes, Tom—good night, and thank you again," Miranda said, holding out her hand; which, after only an instant's hesitation, Tom clasped firmly in his own.

Then, casting a radiant smile towards Nan and Bella, Miranda followed Leo out into the driving rain once more. He did not speak until they had reached Dulcie's caravan; but when Miranda turned to bid him good night, Leo seized both her hands in his, and said quickly, "I'm that glad you're to stay." Then, as quickly, he turned and vanished into the rainy dark.

Breathless, Miranda went inside, where she found both Dulcie and Rosa waiting up for her, wrapped in blankets against the cold; and Dulcie in particular wore an anxious expression. Miranda could only look from one to the other, smiling, until Rosa lost patience. "Out with it, then," she said. "Judging from your face, things couldn't have gone too badly."

"Oh, Rosa, Tom said I could stay!" Miranda exclaimed. "Though if it hadn't been for Bella and Nan, I believe he'd have sent me away tomorrow." And now, impulsively, she threw her arms about Dulcie, who gave her a speechless hug in return.

"That's settled, then," said Rosa. "And I'm not sorry to hear it, Miranda, for all I had doubts at the start. It seems you've made Dulcie happy, and that's worth a good deal by itself."

"Oh yes, and what do you think?" Miranda said to her. "I've brought back the coin to Jemmy. Tom wouldn't have it, and when I told Bella how Jemmy was so fond of it, she said he could keep it for me."

Rosa's manner softened further. "It was kind of you to think of him, Miranda," she said. "I won't forget it. And if I'm cross with you another time, just take no notice."

"There now, I'm glad to see you make friends," said Dulcie. "It's hard enough living in such close quarters, even when there's good will all round."

So Miranda gave the gold coin to Rosa, who closed the sleeping boy's fingers about it again. He stirred a little, but then, tucking his fist beneath his chin, he sighed, and slept peacefully on.

he caravans set out early the next day; and since the heavy rain continued, Leo insisted on driving once more. Apart from a brief halt at another farmhouse, where sufficient food was bought to stave off their hunger, they stopped only when night had fallen, and soon went to their beds.

But looking out of the window the following morning, Miranda saw to her delight that the rain had ceased and a pale blue sky, swept clear save for a few feathery clouds, arched over a vista of wide marshlands, although with this change the weather had grown more bitterly cold than ever. Even Dulcie complained of it, and put on an old overcoat when she went out, having persuaded Leo to let her drive.

While Rosa sat huddled up with Jemmy beneath the bedclothes, Miranda, cloaked in her blankets, remained standing at the window, as the caravans took their way along a road running straight through the marshes. She hoped to catch some glimpse of the sea, but nothing appeared so far except acre upon acre of rushes and grasses and reeds, threaded through with a maze of muddy channels.

Still, there was a briny scent to the air that found its way in around the window; and Miranda fancied it laden with the essence of all she had ever read about the sea—its tempests and shipwrecks, whales and pirates and mermaids—though even now she could hardly believe that today she would see this famous wonder for herself.

She was a little surprised when the caravans turned out of the road to follow a rough track leading towards higher, more uneven ground. The track, moreover, soon came to an end, and after that they lurched across open heath, a waste of grassy tufts and spiny shrubs, with here and there a twisted tree jutting up leafless and forlorn.

"Aren't we nearly to the sea by now?" Miranda asked impatiently.

"It's there all right, beyond those sand hills," Rosa replied, standing to look out herself. "Though we'll stop this side of them, and you'll be glad enough of their shelter."

A distant line of pale hillocks loomed ever higher as the caravans approached; and finally, where the tallest dunes rose above a broad, sandy hollow, the laboring horses were drawn to a halt.

Miranda opened the door and breathed in the cold salt air, at the same time conscious of an unfamiliar rushing murmur everywhere about her. She ran down the steps and, laughing at the feel of the sand beneath her feet, went round to the front of the caravan, where Dulcie had begun to unharness their horse.

"Isn't this a strange place," Miranda exclaimed, looking up the high face of the dune above them. "Could I climb up there? Is the sea at the other side? Oh, Dulcie, is that what I hear, the sound of the waves?"

Dulcie smiled. "Yes, it's the sea at last, Miranda. Of

course, go and look at it if you like, but come back soon. We'll have our work cut out for us, settling in."

Miranda was off in a moment, her feet slithering in the sand as she began to climb. The great dune rose steeply, and she was obliged to clutch at its coarse grasses to keep from slipping back; but before long, gasping and laughing, she had scrambled to the top.

She stood up, and the wind that had fallen tame in the lee of the dune struck full against her, taking her breath away, and bringing tears to her eyes. But there beneath her stretched the curving shoreline, edged with a silver turbulence of foam; while beyond it glittered a spectacle the like of which she had never beheld: the blue immensity of the open sea.

The waves' commotion roared in her ears with a force no less than the wind's, as if striving by sheer din to topple her back. But she stood her ground, exulting in the boundless space of air and water before her. And perhaps because her sight was momentarily glazed with tears, that whole vibrant expanse took on the quality of some unearthly vision; as if the hills and fields and woodlands known to her in the past had been a mere illusory vapor, now in a single instant swept away, so that she gazed as never before on the world's true face.

Its splendor dissolved all limitations, even those of the distant horizon, fusing sea and sky into one immeasurable globe: at the center of which she seemed to be held suspended, no longer sure that the sky did not lie below her, nor the sea above, so far had they lost their accustomed boundaries and become a part of her own giddy perspective.

But then, slowly, she came to herself again; and winking her eyes, found heaven and earth returned to their proper places, vast as ever, but distinct and steady once more, and herself released from their overpowering sway.

She felt cold now, and shrank from the wind. Shaking her head, a bit giddy yet, she turned and descended, sliding and stumbling, to the foot of the dune. The caravans were deserted, the horses already led away to pasture on the nearby heath, and the gypsies gone off in quest of water and firewood. Miranda spied Leo in the distance, walking across the heath with the dog, but Dulcie and Rosa were nowhere to be seen.

As she stood there, of two minds, Bella opened her door and called to her. "Been to look at the sea, have you?" she asked, as Miranda drew near. "The first sight of it's the best—or perhaps you were disappointed?"

"Oh no," Miranda said faintly. "Though it wasn't as I thought it would be; but I can't say how it was, even now."

"You don't seem yourself, my dear," said Bella, regarding her more closely. "Will you come and sit down?"

"No, thank you, Bella," Miranda answered her. "I must find the others—Dulcie said there was work to be done. Though I do feel odd. I think it was looking out over the sea from so high up. I'd never looked at anything in quite that way before."

"Ah, yes," murmured Bella, gazing at Miranda reflectively. But after a moment she said in a brisk voice, "Well, it's no wonder, with nothing to eat all day. But you'll be right enough when we've got the fire going, and a rabbit or two in the pot. Leo's out hunting, and Tom's gone off to the nearest farm with one of the other men, to buy potatoes. There'll be a feast tonight, if we're lucky. Ah, but it's a pity Tom won't play his fiddle as he used to."

Miranda's face lit up at these words. "Did he?" she asked, her old gypsy fancies half inspired again. "And was there dancing as well?"

Bella smiled sadly. "We've not been much for dancing since we came away from the others," she said. "But Tom always played his fiddle before Nan was taken ill. No, he's not had the heart for it lately, but his music was a proper treat in the old days."

"Oh, Bella, don't you think he'd play tonight, for once?" Miranda said wistfully.

"Ah, I don't know, dear," Bella replied. "Only if Nan were to ask, perhaps he might, for her sake. I'll mention it to her, though you mustn't hope too much. She's better today, and if we've a good supper I expect she'll be strong enough to come out afterwards. But now you're looking better yourself, so off you go. Dulcie's most likely fetching water—there's a spring on the heath, just keep straight along and you'll come to it."

So Miranda walked away to the heath, where the ground was firmer and tussocky grass grew mingled with ragged clumps of heather and furze; and at length, descending a short slope, she found the spring, a clear trickle running out over a bent scrap of tin driven into the bank by way of a spout. There was a pail set beneath it to fill, but no sign of anyone nearby.

Having stood indecisive a moment, Miranda sat down to wait in the cold sunlight. However, it was neither Dulcie nor Rosa who presently appeared, but the dog Bruno, with Leo close behind. They both stopped short at the top of the bank, coming upon Miranda so un-expectedly, and she looked up at them speechless.

Then she saw that three rabbits dangled by their heels from Leo's hand, and forgetting her bashfulness, jumped to her feet. "You've already got three!" she exclaimed. "Oh, we'll have a real feast tonight, won't we?"

Leo leapt down the bank, while the dog, a long-legged brown mongrel, ran sniffing up and down the grassy slope. "There's rabbits everywhere, this year," Leo said, his eyes shining as he held out his three towards Miranda, "and Bruno's fast as the wind. He doesn't maul them, either, just gives them a good shake and brings them straight back."

"They're pretty things," said Miranda, stroking the soft, brindled fur of one. "It's a pity they've got to die—but oh, Leo, I'm so hungry, aren't you?"

"Hungry?" Leo laughed. "I could just about eat these three raw—though they'll be better cooked, with potatoes! Besides, we're bound to get more before Bruno's finished, so I'll go along; but we'll meet tonight, at the fire." He gave her a look that set her heart beating faster. Then he whistled to Bruno and strode away, the dog bounding before him.

Miranda sat down again beside the spring, where by now the pail was overflowing. After a little while she heard voices, and Dulcie appeared at the top of the bank, followed by Rosa and Jemmy—the latter two carrying armfuls of sticks, though Dulcie bore a sheaf of long green stalks.

"We wondered where you'd got to," she said to Miranda, coming down the slope.

"And a good thing you're here," added Rosa, descending after her. "We'd have a time carrying all this, and the pail besides."

"Whatever are those green things?" Miranda asked Dulcie, rising and taking up the brimming pail.

"Rushes," Rosa answered for her sister, in a weary voice. "Dulcie spied them growing in a marshy spot back there, and she wouldn't be satisfied until we'd gone and cut some."

"But what are they for?" asked Miranda, puzzled.

Dulcie smiled. "They'll do for making baskets, since there's not much else growing about these parts. And we'd better get on with some new ones tomorrow, if we're to earn our living this winter."

"Do come along with that pail, Miranda," Rosa said impatiently, "it'll be wanted for the pot. And I'm so cold and famished I can hardly stand."

"I saw Leo," Miranda told them as they climbed the bank. "Bruno had caught three rabbits, and they were going after more."

"Well, that's a mercy," said Rosa. "Last time we were here, there weren't so many about."

"Yes, but we'd a different dog before," Dulcie observed. "Here, Miranda, can you manage?" she asked, stopping again, for Miranda had fallen behind, shifting the heavy pail from hand to hand and slopping cold water over her shoes as she did so.

"I'm all right," she replied, "it's just that the handle hurts my fingers."

"Give it here, then," said Dulcie, "and you can take my rushes instead."

"No, I want to do it," Miranda insisted. "You go ahead, and I'll come on more slowly."

So left to herself, Miranda hauled her burden along. By the time she reached the caravans, her arms and hands ached sorely, and her wet feet felt turned to ice; but she carried the pail to the iron pot, already set over a crackling fire, and poured in the water without spilling a single drop.

"There," she pronounced with satisfaction, as though she had performed some remarkable feat, instead of merely carrying a pailful of water from a spring not so very far away. And while there lurked in her mind the unwelcome prospect of weaving baskets on the morrow, she shut it out of her thoughts, and stood warming her stiffened hands at the fire—which would soon set boiling the pot that she herself had helped to fill.

he sun had sunk low over the heath by the time Tom and his companion returned, each carrying a good-sized sack of potatoes.

"I spent every last penny we had," Tom said, depositing his sack beside the fire, "but these'll serve till we've earned something more; and they said there'd be hedging and ditching work at the farm through most of the winter. Leo's coming along," he added. "He'd already got five rabbits, and Bruno was after another. Yes, and I nearly forgot, I've brought this as well." He drew out of his coat pocket a large brown onion. "It cost a penny itself, but I vowed we'd have it."

"Oh, Tom, we've not had an onion in the pot for weeks!" Rosa rejoiced. "Now if only there was a drop of ale, we'd hardly know ourselves."

Bella spoke up with a laugh. "Ale there may not be, but I've tea enough for us all—and it'll warm our bones better than ale tonight."

There followed a great bustle on every hand. The potatoes were scrubbed, the onion was chopped up, and a kettleful of water put aside for the tea. In the midst of these preparations Leo returned with six fat rabbits, which Dulcie and some of the others set about skinning and cleaning, while Bruno yelped eagerly for his reward of innards and other remains.

Much to her relief, Miranda was not asked to help with

the rabbits, as the very sight of their naked carcasses made her shudder. Nevertheless, like Bruno, she could scarcely wait for her supper; and the others must have felt the same way, for while the pot bubbled and steamed they sat very still about the fire, even the children speaking only an occasional word or two.

But at long last the stew was judged to be ready, and generous portions of meat and potatoes and morsels of onion were ladled out, glistening with savory broth. As all fell to eating, there descended upon them a silence deeper than ever; and only after every plate was empty, and the tea was brewed, did they seem to regain the power of speech.

Then, however, there arose such a cheerful clamor among these gypsies as Miranda had not heard before, while Jemmy and the few other children ran about laughing in the shadows beyond the fire. Even Rosa joked with everyone, in the best of humors; and after a time she went up to Tom and linked her arm through his, saying to him in a sweetly beguiling voice, "Tom, dear, won't you please bring out your fiddle tonight? It's been such a long time since you've played—indeed, I hope you haven't forgotten how."

The others laughed, and Tom smiled at his sister kindly; but then his face grew sober again. "Nay, you know I won't play without Nan," he said. "I'm sorry to disappoint you, Rosa, but for all our feasting, I haven't the heart." And turning away, he left the fire and walked off alone into the shadows.

"Rosa, I'm surprised at you," Dulcie rebuked her. "You've spoilt his evening now, with thinking only of yourself."

"But, Dulcie," Miranda volunteered, "when I saw Bella earlier, she said Nan might come out after supper. Shall I go and ask?"

Dulcie appeared uncertain; but Rosa's face, which had grown sulky at her sister's words, brightened at once. "Yes, Miranda, do," she urged.

So Miranda hastened away and tapped at Bella's door, which the old woman opened directly. "Ah, I know what you've come about," she said, laughing, "and I'm happy to tell you that Nan's just wrapping up, ready to come out. As soon as I mentioned we'd spoken of Tom's music, she seemed to feel stronger. So run and tell him he'd better fetch down his fiddle, since Nan's particularly asked for it."

Even as Miranda hurried away, she met Tom walking slowly towards the caravans. "Oh, Tom," she cried breathlessly, "Nan's just coming, and she wants to hear you play—so won't you, please?"

Tom stopped, and regarded her grimly. "She's got up, has she?" he asked. "Aye, but is she fit to be out, that's the question—" He broke off, staring past Miranda, who turned to see Bella already assisting Nan down the steps.

Tom walked up to them, and stood in their way. "Not so fast, my girl," he said to his wife. "It's cold, and the night air's harmed you before. You'd best go back, or you'll find yourself worse off than ever."

Nan stood her ground. "Nay, even if I am, it'll be worth

it," she said, her dark eyes glittering. "It's been far too long since you've played, and I believe the sound of it would do me good."

Tom stared at her; but suddenly he laughed, and threw an arm about her shoulders. "Fever or no, it's clear you've still a mind of your own," he said. "Very well, then. I expect it'll do us all good to forget our troubles for a bit. Yes, by heaven, that fiddle's been gathering dust in its cupboard long enough."

By the time Miranda had accompanied the two women to the fire, and Nan was comfortably settled near its warmth, Tom was back again, carrying a worn black case. While everyone looked on, he removed the instrument, itself well-kept and gleaming; and after a few moments' work of plucking strings and twisting pegs, he tightened up the bow, and tucked the fiddle beneath his chin.

Then such extraordinary music floated out upon the cold, firelit darkness as Miranda had never heard, or even imagined. It seemed a music as bright as the fire, yet as full of embracing shadows as the night itself: a music both glad and sorrowful, as if, in its harmonious contradictions, it laughed and wept at one and the same time.

And while Miranda listened, letting her eyes stray round the fire, it struck her that Tom's fiddle was singing of the mingled griefs and joys these gypsies knew themselves. For despite their every care and affliction, their faces tonight shone bright with pleasure; and although there was no dancing, and their clothes were not only faded and patched but barely sufficient to keep them warm, in spirit they seemed to dance as gaily as those others in Miranda's picture book, arrayed in all their silk and velvet and gold.

And at last she saw the truth of these gypsies' lives: a truth both simpler and more profound than ever she had conceived. They were, undeniably, a band of shabby vagrants, who reckoned their wealth in pennies rather than gold; yet the very hardships and ignominies they suffered had taught them courage and strength, and endowed them thus with a beauty surpassing the glitter and flourish of her most extravagant dreams.

Nor was that beauty lacking in Leo himself, though it might belie the alien glamour in which she had clothed him; though his lean brown face and hands might owe as much to scanty food and rough weather as to his gypsy blood. But Miranda could see in his eyes the same undaunted spirit as shone in all the others': a spirit only the nobler for arising out of conditions so humble, and qualities so plain.

And now this truth about Leo endeared him to her the more. She found it to be not merely sufficient but far better than her ignorant flights of fancy: and in that moment she knew that she truly loved him.

As she gazed at him across the fire, filled with a strange sort of wonder, Leo smiled; and soon afterwards, getting up quietly, came round to sit beside her. And though he spoke no word, Miranda found his presence both stirring and comfortable—not unlike that of the fire itself, whose flames had sunk by now to a steady flickering above its settled coals.

Tom's music also seemed a little diminished; and presently, drawing the bow over the strings in a final sweep, he lowered his fiddle again, with a smile at once weary and triumphant. There was a brief silence, and then a burst of applause. Nan gave him a kiss, so did Bella, and the others gathered round to thank him as well.

Miranda, when it came her turn, only put out her hand, unable to express her gratitude for all that had filled her mind while he played. But Nan, at his side, spoke up. "You know, Tom, it was Miranda who first asked for your music tonight. In fact, it's because of her that I came to ask you myself."

"Well, missy, it seems you've got the better of me once again," Tom said with a grin. "But mind now, there's work to be done tomorrow, and no more goings-on like tonight's for a good long time."

Then the gypsies retired to their beds; and while they slept, the fire dwindled away to darkness and a heap of cold ashes. But all night the sea murmured distantly in Miranda's ears, like an echo of some departed music: a music whose sound, though stilled itself, had set the waters reverberating in endless refrain.

ext morning Miranda woke to find the skies overcast and a damp chill in the air that seemed to creep into her very marrow. Aware of some cheerless cloud upon her mind as well, she soon recognized it to be the threat of basketmaking; and sure enough, after a meal of thin broth made from the bones of the rabbits, Dulcie bade Miranda sit down upon the ground with the bundle of rushes brought home the previous day.

They were of two different kinds, one slender and pliant, the other sturdier and more rigid; and Miranda's first task was to divide them up. When this was done, Dulcie chose some of each, and laid them out before her.

"See, dear," she said, "just take a dozen or so of the stouter sort and make two groups of them, and cross one over the other. Then bind round them at the center, this way, and afterwards spread out the ends, like the spokes of a wheel." She next went on to explain how the weaker rushes must be woven through the spokes, drawn under and over, and round and round, until the base of the basket was completed.

"Now I'll begin another myself," Dulcie said, "while you go on with this one." And turning aside, she left Miranda fumbling with the slippery green stalks, which seemed already determined to arrange themselves into the wrong shape. After a lengthy struggle she ended with a most lopsided affair, its spokes slanted askew and pitiful spaces left in their windings—at the sight of which Dulcie laughed merrily, and said she had better begin again.

By now Miranda's fingers were so cold and stiff that they scarcely seemed her own. Her second attempt proved no more successful than the first, and she grew close to tears, not only because of the ache in her fingers and the contrary ways of the rushes, but in mortification over her stupidity.

What a blockhead Dulcie must think her, though she was far too kind to say so; while Rosa, who would soon be returning from the spring, was sure to express a less sympathetic opinion. Besides, there was still the chance that if she failed to do her work properly, Tom might send her away; and perhaps worse yet was her fear that Leo would think very poorly of her indeed if she could not learn this simple art, known to every gypsy woman in the camp.

But forcing back her tears, she pulled her work apart once more and began afresh. By the time Rosa and Jemmy appeared, she had made a better start; at least the spokes were more evenly spaced, and there were not so many gaps in the rushes wound about them. Rosa, however, only glanced briefly at Miranda's latest effort, saying, "Never mind if you spoil a few to begin with. You're bound to do better in time." And with a half-suppressed smile, she carried her pail away to the fire.

After that, Miranda had little heart to continue. But by good luck she was spared further suffering just then, for Tom announced that the morning's tide had cast up a quantity of driftwood, which they must make haste to gather in. Miranda put aside her work with alacrity, and followed after the others as they trooped to the beach, skirting the high dune she had climbed the day before.

This morning, however, the sea wore a very different aspect. Surveyed on its own level, it appeared to have lost some of its magnitude, and the waves that had fringed it with silver now rose gray and dark, to fall scrambling untidily among the tangled seaweed at their edge, leaving behind a dull brown froth as they slid away. Nevertheless, its uproar was unabated; the wind sweeping across the sands added its strident voice to the clamor of the waves, and somehow Miranda felt her recent humiliations eased by their rough endurance.

Then she found no more time for her own concerns. Turning to the scattered wrack of broken boards and staves and derelict branches, she worked as hard as anyone else at dragging these prizes up the beach. In less than an hour every scrap had been heaped beyond the farthest reach of the tide; but next commenced the more wearisome labor of carrying everything through the dunes, which took them the better part of the afternoon, and rain had begun to fall before the last fragment was stowed away beneath the caravans to dry.

Miranda and Dulcie were both very wet by the time they got home. Even though Rosa had taken Jemmy back earlier, and lighted the stove, Miranda could not stop shivering, and her spirits sank at the thought that there could be no fire out of doors tonight. Instead, Dulcie set a pot of water on the stove to boil, since Leo had gone out hunting again and brought every caravan several pieces of rabbit to be cooked.

"Rabbit today, and rabbit tomorrow, and it'll be everlasting rabbit all the winter," said Rosa drearily. "What I wouldn't give for a mouthful of mutton, just once."

"Nay, but we can buy some fish in the town," Dulcie reminded her. "And tomorrow's market day, if we'd want to go."

"Yes, and a poor excuse for a market it is, I remember," Rosa scoffed. "Mainly a lot of fishermen's wives selling a few sprats they don't want themselves. Though I'd be glad of some fish for a change," she admitted. "We'll go, then, if the weather clears—I shouldn't much fancy pushing that barrow half a dozen miles in the rain."

"Oh, may I come with you, too?" Miranda asked.

"No, dear, I think not," Dulcie replied. "They may have got word of you there by now, and if so, they'll be looking over any gypsies for something out of the way. Besides, you'd better have another try at your baskets."

Thus, next morning, Miranda was left behind, while her friends, taking Jemmy along, with one or two other women who had wares of their own to sell, set off early for the town. The rain had let up; and as an intermittent sunlight shone between heavy clouds, the sand about the caravans soon dried off, so that Miranda could find no excuse to delay bringing out those tiresome rushes and setting to work again.

But although she was resolved not to lose patience, and found herself more at ease with neither Dulcie's nor Rosa's eyes upon her, the rushes proved just as intractable as before, and rather than gaining in skill, her fingers seemed clumsier than ever.

Again Miranda grew close to tears. Yet she could not very well leave the work undone, and have nothing to show for her labors when Dulcie and Rosa came home that night; so, torn between obstinacy and despair, she wearily unraveled her first misshapen attempt, and had begun binding together the central rushes once more, when she heard someone call her name, and looked up to find Bella walking towards her.

"I've been watching you through my window," she said, "and I couldn't bear to see you start over. You've tried your best, dear, and I'll answer for it to Dulcie tonight. But put these things away now, and I'll tell your fortune."

"Oh, Bella, will you?" Miranda cried, jumping to her feet. "I've been hoping you would—I haven't forgotten what you said the other day. And perhaps I'll even learn why I make such a muddle of things," she added ruefully, beginning to gather up the rushes strewn in disorder on the ground.

"Perhaps you may, at that," said Bella with a smile. "Come along, we'll go into your own caravan, and have an hour or so to ourselves."

hen they had sat down together on one of the bunks, Bella brought out from under her shawl a small packet, wrapped in a red silk cloth and tied about with a silken cord. Unfastening these, she revealed a pack of cards, shabby with use, their backs patterned with a fine crosshatching so faded that it could scarcely be distinguished.

"These cards are very old," she said. "They belonged to my grandmother, and they were given to her by another gypsy woman, said to be a witch—when folk believed more in such things. I daresay it was only because she had the sight; though my grandmother had it as well."

"Dulcie told me you've the sight yourself, Bella," Miranda said, now slightly awed by the old woman despite her matter-of-fact way of speaking.

"It's true, I've seen a good many things in the cards that have come about," Bella replied. "But I haven't my grandmother's gift for visions. Why, she could look in her crystal and tell you what was happening far away that moment, or make out events not to take place for years to come. While I've never been able to see much in the crystal but a sort of mist, that never takes on a clear shape as it did for her.

"So I've mainly kept to the cards," she went on, shuffling up the pack in her wrinkled brown hands. "They have their own laws; and if something beyond them comes to me while I'm reading them, it's still the cards that guide me, almost as if they spoke to me in my mind. Well then," she proceeded, fitting the pack together again, "we've first to choose the card that stands for yourself. And that's easy enough, as it's plain you're meant to be the Queen of Coins—you've only to ask Jemmy about that!"

Sorting through the pack until she found the appropriate card, she laid it face up on the bed between them. It showed a woman, regally robed, bearing a scepter in one hand and a great gold disk in the other.

"She looks very grand to be me," said Miranda.

"All women are queens to the cards," Bella assured her, smiling. "Now, my dear, take the rest in your hands and mix them together, so they've got your touch on them. That's it, now halve them—once, and twice, and three times. Good. Now I'll have them back."

Miranda did as she was told, if somewhat awkwardly. The cards felt warm to her hands, perhaps from Bella's own touch; but she also fancied the touch of others upon them, Bella's grandmother, and that gypsy witch, and perhaps others unknown to Bella herself.

The old woman then began laying out the topmost cards, face down, about the central figure of the Queen. One beneath her, one to the left, one above her, and one to the right; three in a row beneath all these, one below the three, and another below that, making an end.

"Now, Miranda," Bella said to her, with greater solemnity than before, "I'll turn them up, one at a time, and tell you something of each. But they'll say something further, read as a whole, so we'll also see what they amount to in the end."

Then Bella turned over the card at the feet of the Queen, and she laughed outright. "There, to be sure, it's the Fool," she exclaimed. "You might have called him up yourself, with your talk of muddles. This first card's at the heart of your life, my dear, set there in the midst of the others. And do you see how the Fool goes waltzing along with his dog at the top of a cliff, as if he hadn't any idea of the danger lying before him? Well, I expect that's how you've been yourself, not having seen your way clear as yet, and apt to be a little rash and thoughtless—or, as you might say, muddleheaded.

"But you mustn't take it amiss," she added quickly, "for the Fool's a great deceiver. Just when folk think to laugh at him, he plays them a trick and shows himself wiser than anyone else. Yes, I'd take heart at the Fool, especially as this card's the first; for he'll lead you on through the rest, and perhaps teach you a trick or two of your own."

Miranda remained silent, abashed, yet privately hoping she was not such a fool as this silly fellow, in his cap and bells and garish coat of patches, who tripped so blithely towards the brink of certain death.

"Now then, we'll see what's next," said Bella, turning over the card to the left of the Queen. It showed a man in a wide-brimmed hat, flourishing a wand over a table scattered with numerous objects, cups and curved daggers and little balls of various colors.

"This speaks very well for you, dear," Bella asserted. "It's the Magician, or the Juggler, as he's sometimes called. He's standing ready to work his arts on those jumbled things before him, and bring them to order; and it means you're blessed with some art or skill of your own, even though you may not know it as yet."

"I certainly don't," returned Miranda wryly, thinking of her baskets again.

"Ah, but the cards know you better than you know yourself," said Bella. "You may be in for a surprise one of these days."

Miranda only smiled, far from sure that the old woman was not mistaken; but she listened attentively as Bella turned over the card above the Queen.

"Ah, see now, there's the Star," she exclaimed. "The maiden who pours out the waters of life from two pitchers —as you've already brought new life to poor Dulcie, haven't you? Not to mention leading Tom to play his fiddle again. Still, there's more to it than just that. It's a card of new beginnings, too, and the stars set there in the sky stand for the spirit, and things beyond the earth. There's something greater to come, if I'm not mistaken, so we'll go on at once—as the next card says more of your future."

But to Miranda's alarm, that card, turned up to the right of the Queen, bore the figure of Death: a skeleton wielding a scythe over a newly sprouted field, surrounded by a litter of severed heads and hands.

"It appears there's some tremendous change in store

for you, Miranda," Bella told her soberly. "Though it's not as ill as it looks—it needn't mean you're soon to die, or anything as terrible as that. No, it's more a season of trials, and an overturning of the past. You'll find your life made very different, and you'll want all your strength to see you through a time of darkness."

Miranda tried not to feel discouraged. But so far the cards had told her very little she could make sense of, nor had they offered any hint of the sign for which she hoped so dearly.

Now Bella, looking a bit puzzled herself, turned up the three cards laid in a row beneath these others; and at once her face cleared. "Here are your trials, then, plain as day," she stated. "King of Cups, turned head-to-foot; Queen of Swords, the grieving woman; and see there, it's your Knave of Wands at last." And she gave Miranda a significant glance.

"Now, these are matters to be settled before the rest will come right," she said. "That King's very likely your father; and as the card's reversed, it seems he's done wrong, or some misfortune's befallen him. And the Queen's doubtless your mother, holding the sword of loss—though whether she's grieving for you, or for another, it's difficult to say. But there at the end's your young man, the Knave, with his traveler's staff. He's known as the stranger with good intentions, and he's one to be trusted—even though these first two appear to stand in his way. Yes, and there must be some further trouble about him, perhaps some difference between the

Knave and yourself, not soon to be resolved. But he's there, for all that, my dear, the very one you've been thinking of."

Miranda looked up to find Bella regarding her with a clear and kindly gaze. "Your heart and your fate agree," she said, "and there's nothing can keep them apart in the end, even if there's a long road to travel before they're one. But perhaps we'll learn something more about that in the last two cards."

She turned over the first of those that remained. "This stands for the root of the matter, as the Fool was the heart," she said, "and see, it's your gold again, the Ace of Coins. It's a very favorable card, my dear; not just prosperity, and happy conclusions, but higher attainments as well. I wonder—" An extraordinary look came into Bella's eyes; but then, with a slight shake of her head, she continued.

"We'll see the last one now, and the deepest," she said. "This card is the truth that's been hidden beneath the others. It lies in the dark of the earth, and nourishes the root, and the heart, and the branches of all the other cards—as you see how they're laid out to make a sort of tree?"

Miranda nodded, unable to speak, for Bella's manner held a new intensity. Then she turned over the card; and for some time afterwards said nothing at all. Miranda looked at her expectantly, but the old woman appeared to have fallen into a sort of trance, staring before her fixedly, her lips moving in soundless words.

At length she stirred, as though brought back to her

senses. Still she said nothing, but only reached out and took Miranda's hand, turning it over to look at the palm; and then took hold of the other, and did the same. Loosing them again, after a moment or two, she looked up at Miranda, her dark eyes luminous, and finally spoke.

"Yes, it's in both your hands as well," she said softly, "and in the light of the other cards, this last can only point to one end. Though I hardly know how to explain it, Miranda, so you'll believe me. For it's even deeper than I'd expected, and far stranger, I'm sure, than ever you've dreamed yourself."

"But what does the card mean?" Miranda asked, unsure whether to feel encouraged or apprehensive. "All I see is a woman wearing a veil and a crown, and holding a book."

"She's the High Priestess, my dear," Bella said reverently, "and even taken alone, she's the card of uncommon wisdom. But read along with those others, the Fool and the Magician, the Star, and Death, and the Ace of Coins, she's a sign of some remarkable awakening in store for you.

"And beyond that, I saw something else just now," she went on, her voice fallen nearly to a whisper. "I saw you, Miranda, wearing the veil and the crown of the High Priestess—as I've only known the same vision granted once before. It was my grandmother told me of it, and it was seen by the old woman who gave her the cards. For she saw my grandmother crowned High Priestess, in just the same way, as the sign of her own gift—that is to say, the sight."

"But, Bella, you can't mean I've got the sight myself," Miranda protested, laughing. "Why, I can't even tell if the weather's to change, from one day to the next!"

"That's as may be," Bella answered her. "I said you'd not believe it, didn't I? But that's what I saw; and even if I hadn't, the cards speak plainly enough. I've never in all my days seen these particular cards turn up together in one reading; and in this order, especially, they speak as if they'd a single voice, telling the very same thing. But mind you," she added, "there's troubles to be met. In fact, I believe your gift may be the obstacle I spoke of, that'll stand between you and your young man until some later time."

"Oh dear, I don't understand it," cried Miranda. "How could I have the sight and not know it? Why, I don't even know properly what it means, or what it is I'm expected to see!"

"Ah, my dear, the sight takes in all the world—high and low, near and far, past, present, and future. Sometimes one part's clearer than another, or sometimes you might be given to see the whole of the world at once. But it's not something to be explained in words. You'll only begin to understand it when it comes to you, little by little, and you find out these things for yourself."

"But how shall I ever find them out?" Miranda asked helplessly. "For I'm the same as I was before. I've not been turned into a High Priestess by magic, no matter what the cards may say. Why, I'm still just a girl, and not even a true gypsy. And what should I do with such a gift, if I've really got it?"

"I believe Dulcie told me you once asked to learn fortune-telling," the old woman said, with a humorous glint in her eye. "Well, now it appears you spoke better than you knew. In fact, you must have seen something of the future to have such an idea come into your head."

"But, Bella, that wasn't how it happened," Miranda insisted. "I was only remembering some silly tale about gypsies I'd seen in a book years ago."

"Ah, but you did remember it, didn't you?" Bella returned quietly. "Silly or not, it led you here, to the cards, where the truth was waiting. And now your way's made clear."

"But it isn't," objected Miranda. "I can't see my way a bit."

"Perhaps that's because it's very simple," Bella said soothingly. "You've only to begin by learning the cards yourself; though I've no doubt you'll go beyond my own powers one day, as it appears you've the gift given whole, while I've only some part of it. Don't be discouraged, my dear. If you're a stranger to your sight, it's because you've not known how to make use of it. For it's an art, as well as a gift. It's got to be cultivated like any other; but I'll teach you all that I'm able to, and gladly."

"But what about Dulcie and Rosa?" Miranda asked anxiously. "Won't they feel hurt if I'm to learn fortune-telling now, instead of baskets?"

"There's no reason why you can't do both," Bella replied. "I'll explain everything to Dulcie, and to Tom as well, so he'll know what you're about—though you may find it hard at first. There may be those who'll disbelieve your gift, or misunderstand it. But Dulcie's sure to uphold you, as of course I'll do myself."

Taking Miranda's hands in her own, Bella held them fast for a moment; and Miranda felt that there passed between them a swift current of warmth, and strength, and an impulse more profound: as though in Bella's hands Miranda's were clasped by those of all the others who had possessed the gift before them, through countless ages past.

Then, releasing her hands again, Bella began to gather up the cards; and having retied their silk cloth, she took her leave, with only a simple word of farewell.

Miranda spent the rest of the day wandering about the camp, her mind in a whirl. She still could not bring herself to believe what Bella had told her, and the more she considered them, the more strangely the old woman's words echoed in her head. She spoke little to anyone throughout supper; and when Leo, sitting nearby, chaffed her good-naturedly about her silence, she met his eyes with difficulty, and could hardly muster a smile in return.

It was late that night when Dulcie and the others came back from the town. They were in cheerful spirits, having made money enough to buy bread, and candles, and even a quantity of small fish—which were skewered and grilled there and then over the last flames of the fire.

But afterwards Miranda saw Bella draw Dulcie aside. Not daring to witness their conversation, she fled to her caravan, where she found Rosa settling Jemmy in bed. "How did you get on with the baskets, then?" Rosa asked, glancing up as she entered.

Miranda only stood before her tongue-tied, until Rosa laughed. "I suppose it was the same story as before," she said amicably. "Ah, well, don't fret—you'll learn in time, if you put your mind to it; and tomorrow I'll give you a lesson myself."

Filled with a greater confusion than ever, Miranda could think of no possible way to explain the matter. And she was relieved, when Dulcie came in with a peculiar look on her face, that she said nothing about her talk with Bella, but only laid her hand gently upon Miranda's head, telling her to make haste to sleep, as the hour was very late.

n the days that followed, rather than growing accustomed to the idea of her unsuspected gift, Miranda only found herself the more bewildered, and at times felt that she hardly knew who she was any longer, or whether she stood on her feet or her head.

For one thing, whatever Bella had told Dulcie—or she, in turn, had said to Rosa—there were marked changes in both sisters' behavior. Dulcie, always somewhat protective, was now grown more than ever solicitous, no longer asking Miranda's help with even the simplest task; whereas Rosa seemed to have reverted to her earlier mistrust, and seldom favored her with a word if she could help it.

The news of her distinction spread rapidly among the other gypsies as well; and while before they had begun to treat Miranda as one of themselves, now they returned to glancing at her with a mixture of curiosity and deference. Tom appeared altogether baffled by the whole affair, and would offer her only a brief nod in greeting, or sometimes an ironic lift of the eyebrows—as though Miranda had played them all some sort of trick, the nature of which he could not make out.

But worse than everything else, Leo had taken to avoiding her, and refused to meet her eye if their paths chanced to cross. It was clear that, with a sense of chagrin even deeper than Tom's perplexity, or Rosa's doubt, he felt himself betrayed. Yet his look was not so much offended as downcast. He would roam the heath for hours with Bruno, though his former pleasure in hunting appeared quite lost, and come home to brood all evening over the fire, silent and withdrawn.

Miranda grieved as much for Leo as for herself. But how could she protest that her feelings towards him were unchanged, when they had never been openly declared; or expect him to see that she was unaltered, when others treated her in such an altered manner themselves? Since only Nan, aside from Bella—and Jemmy, who knew no better—regarded Miranda entirely as before; and Nan so seldom left her bed, as winter came on and the weather grew colder, that her influence was little felt about the camp.

In the end, it was only Bella's confidence and encouragement that kept Miranda from despair. For the old woman behaved as if nothing out of the ordinary had occurred, and even when she began to teach Miranda the cards, her attitude was no more enigmatic than Dulcie's had been towards basketwork.

Indeed, Miranda wondered at the commonplace fashion in which Bella conducted their sessions together, having expected some far more unusual sort of instruction by which her hidden gift, if in truth she possessed it, might be awakened to magical visions all at once. But instead, her lessons, held in Bella's caravan for an hour or two every day, consisted only of learning the cards' broadest interpretations; and in none of their curious ranks and characters did she find anything beyond an array of cryptic images, whose meanings it sorely taxed her wits to remember.

Even when she proved to have forgotten much of what she had been taught the day before, Bella would only smile, and begin again. But Miranda's heart grew increasingly heavy, and sometimes she dreaded her hours with the cards as much as she had her lessons in weaving.

Besides, after they were over for the day, she had nowhere else to turn for companionship, troubled no less by Dulcie's anxious concern than she was by Rosa's chilly silences. She took to wandering away from the camp, walking restlessly across the heath, or else, more often, beside the sea, where few of the gypsies went themselves unless a storm tide left behind a further supply of driftwood. And in the end she found that solitude a better consolation than any company. The sky's wintry pall reflected in the leaden waters suited her mournful broodings very well; while every wave that slumped defeated upon the sand seemed fraught with a weariness equal to her own.

Yet even that solace was brief, at best; and night after night she went to her bed thwarted and dispirited by another day of failures, only to find the cards' ambiguous faces woven evasively through her dreams.

As the winter wore on, however, Miranda discovered that Bella's patience was to be rewarded. For the cards, which had always seemed strewn about her mind in a nonsensical jumble, slowly began to sort themselves out and to exhibit a clearer scheme: as though they had been the leaves torn from a book, hopelessly scattered and mixed, but wherein, once gathered up into their proper order, the tale they told could at last be read. So that now, even when the cards were shuffled again, their true pattern remained fixed in Miranda's head; and those identities and meanings over which she had labored so long and painfully seemed almost trivial, compared to her wider vision of their whole design.

Nevertheless, that word "vision" was still to Miranda nothing more than a figure of speech. Even if she could decipher the cards with some degree of competence, she saw no further beyond them than before; and thus, rather than feeling encouraged, she began to doubt her powers more seriously than ever. If they would not be called forth now, when she had learned their outward signs, and shown herself ready to make use of them, how should they reveal themselves thereafter? And although Bella counseled her to bide her time, she only grew more restless and impatient, and at last thoroughly disgusted with the entire matter.

Then, early one morning, Miranda awoke to a curious sense of change. At first she could not imagine what it meant; but when she got up and stepped outside the caravan, she found the answer to be, quite simply, that the earth had turned a little towards spring.

She had almost forgotten that spring would come, so heavily had that winter's darkness seemed to weigh upon her spirits and the world about her. But today, while the heath lay brown and bleak as before, the air was grown mild, and the wind blew softly, laden with scents of thawed soil and stirring vegetation. She felt her heart grow lighter, in spite of its every burden; and at the same time there came over her a desire to look at the sea, to find out whether it, too, had emerged from winter's long shadow.

Without a word to anyone, she hurried off through the dunes; and her hopes were not to be disappointed, for this morning the sea was transmuted to a deep and lucent indigo, the sun's bright disk strewn gold across its rippled swell. The dark veil of winter had fallen away, baring this watery face alive and alight, as with sudden laughter —as though the sea had laughed all the while behind a sober disguise, but now came forth, its season of mourning past, and revealed its perennial mirth.

Yet she divined in that laughter something other than mere rejoicing; there was a certain mockery, too, as if the sea were laughing at some joke or secret which Miranda could not fathom. The more she strove to make sense of this mystery, the more it confounded and befuddled her, much as the cards had done when she pored over them so long that their figures dissolved into an absurd confusion.

For now the waves' dancing reflections seemed to set her a lesson of their own, even while they dazzled her eyes, and turned her head as giddy as on that day when she had looked out over the sea for the first time. She felt herself grow ever more light-headed, until the world about her appeared to fall away—unless it was she who was raised above it, and suspended once again at a great height: from which there was nothing to be seen but an endless golden brilliance, absorbing the diverse and variegated matters of water and earth and sky, and refining them away to invisible presences, like imperceptible motes of dust giving substance to its pure illumination.

Still, while her dazzled sight was blind to all but this formless brilliance, Miranda could somehow perceive, as if through other eyes, the myriad forms of which it consisted. Not only the sun's fire, the flashing waters, the crystalline sands, but images less exalted as well: the dunes' weathered and rusted grasses, the broken sticks and ragged seaweed stranded by the waves—even, by some trick of recall, those waves as they had lain so long obscured and dulled by winter's leaden shroud.

And then at last Miranda understood. For she saw the sea in all of its guises at once: in its wayward surfaces, which darkened or brightened, mourned or rejoiced, according to the seasons and weathers of the earth; yet also in its subtler character, its part in this single embracing radiance, which stood beyond earthly conditions and was eternally the same.

Nor was this radiant gold divided from the sea's dappled fluctuations, but dwelt, innate and essential, hidden within them, even as the sea invisibly suffused that sheer, unalterable light. And this was the riddle at which the sea had laughed: that each of these opposite truths was held concealed in the other; and that neither could be fully known until both were seen as one.

Now Miranda laughed out loud herself—and at once her laughter brought her back to the sea's edge, where she stood gazing on the waves as before. As though she had gazed on the sea all along, instead of into some rare, ethereal realm. As though there were no difference between the two: which was, in the end, the deepest truth of her vision.

And a vision she knew it to be, if not bestowed on her in any manner she might have expected, having shown her no portents of the future, no glimpses of distant events. Yet, in beholding earth and heaven so mingled, she had sensed all places and times to be interfused—as though, by some small effort, she might have fixed her sight on any location or moment she chose, so closely bound together were the vast and the particular, the remote and the immediate, within the coherent compass of their whole.

For the present, however, restored to her everyday senses, Miranda was content to turn and move slowly away from the sea. Though its laughter remained in her ears as she walked back between the dunes, smiling a little at the joke it had shared with her, and all that its mysterious waters had disclosed.

he went straight to Bella's caravan and tapped at the door. Bella soon opened it, and her eyes widened at the sight of Miranda's face.

"I've been to the sea, Bella," she said eagerly, "and I saw it laughing; and then I saw why it was laughing, too. Oh dear, that sounds ridiculous, doesn't it?"

"Nay, I think not," replied Bella, with a grave smile. "But there's more to be said, if I understand you rightly. Come away, my dear. We'll walk on the heath, and you'll tell me about it there."

It was early still, and the heath lay quiet and empty save for the horses grazing over its dry tussocks. Bella took Miranda's arm as they walked along, each silent with her own thoughts. But when they had gone a little distance, Bella stopped and, turning to face Miranda, spoke at last.

"Now then. Why was the sea laughing?" she asked.

"Well," Miranda began, "at first it was only because the sun was out, and the winter was gone. But somehow there was a joke at the back of it, and the sea was laughing at that as well; and even laughing at me, for not seeing the joke myself. But then"—and she looked into Bella's eyes—"I did see it, after all."

"Ah, did you, indeed?" said Bella softly. "And how did you come to do so?"

"To tell you the truth, Bella," Miranda answered shyly,

"I think it must have been a sort of vision. Because I seemed to be seeing things in two ways at the same time—the way they'd always looked, and another way, like a great light, that was a part of them, and they were a part of it, because they were really one. And that was the joke I hadn't seen before—that each was there in the other all along. Oh, it sounds such nonsense, put into words. But do you understand it a little?"

"I understand it very well," Bella replied seriously. "And you may be sure that it was a vision, my dear. You've found your sight at last, and it's everything I'd hoped for you, and more."

"But how could it come about that way, without my even trying?" Miranda asked.

"Ah, but you've been working at it," Bella answered her with a smile. "Even when you only learned the meanings of the cards. Even when you thought none of it was any use, and I was just a silly old woman filling your head with a pack of lies."

Miranda blushed at these words. "I'm sorry, Bella," she murmured. "Though, really, I didn't always think so—and it was only because I was so unhappy, and felt such a fool."

"Fool you may have been," said Bella, "but fool you were bound to be, as your own cards showed. For, as I told you then, the Fool's both foolish and wise at once. He's got two sides to him, just as you've got yourself, though sometimes one's to be seen, and sometimes the other. And he's always laughing at those who can't see the whole of him—just as you said the sea was laughing for the same reason. It's the same joke, the Fool's and the sea's; and it's your own joke, too; for it was the other side of yourself you saw at last, the one that was hidden away."

"I suppose that's true," Miranda said slowly, "though I don't feel much wiser even now. I've got so many troubles, and I don't in the least know what to do about them."

"Perhaps that's because you haven't seen them in the proper light," Bella returned. "But I think you'll begin to, after today. Besides, I've some new lessons for you now," she added. "I've been keeping them until you were ready, as they'd only have discouraged you worse before. We'll go back, shall we? And I'll explain. In fact, I've something in particular to tell you, now that this day has come."

Thus, they retraced their steps across the heath—which now appeared to Miranda touched by some lingering reflection of her vision; as if its wilderness of wasted grass and gorse rejoiced, as the sea had done, to find the weather so fine and warm, and laughed in the secret knowledge of saps and leaves and golden flowerings already astir beneath their drab disguises.

Returned to Bella's caravan, where Nan was still asleep, the old woman bade Miranda sit down; and taking hold of both her hands, she turned them over to look at the palms once more. Then, with a nod of satisfaction, she released them, and began to speak in a low voice.

"You've come to your sight at last, my dear, as one of the few to be so gifted. And now you're truly joined to the others gone before you—just as though you were bound to them by flesh and blood. But there's a further bond as well, between yourself and those of your kind. In the way of that kinship, you've been given another name, as they were all given such names, to stand for that side of them blessed with the sight. And it's fallen to me to tell you your own today. It was long ago, when I saw you wearing the veil and the crown, that I heard it spoken; but now you're ready to hear it yourself. Bend close, and listen—I'll say it only once."

Then Miranda, putting her head next to Bella's, heard the old woman pronounce the name: *Mira*.

In the silence that followed, Miranda seemed to hear those syllables echoing over some endless distance, as though whispered in turn by other voices, farther and farther away, until, in the end, distinct yet infinitely remote, they were uttered for the last time. Or else, as it also seemed, for the first: as if pronounced by the original power whose gift that *Mira* was to bestow.

Miranda looked up, and sighed. "Thank you, Bella," she said quietly. "I'm glad you were the one to tell me. How odd, though—it's very like my other name, isn't it? As though it was hidden there all the while."

"Yes, and there's more to it," Bella replied. "For it's also the name of a star in the heavens, a peculiar star that's set at the heart of the Whale. Indeed, its very name means the Wonder, as sometimes it's bright enough to be seen, and sometimes it fades away and vanishes altogether. Now that's another lesson for you to think on.

And talking of lessons, I've something to show you before you go."

The old woman got up, and opening a cupboard, where Miranda saw that Tom's fiddle case was put away, she brought out a box and placed it in Miranda's hands. It was made of some heavy dark wood, carved all over with leafy tendrils apparently forming a simple pattern, but proving on closer inspection to be twined in a maze of intricate knots.

Bella told her to raise the lid; and there, upon a lining of dark blue velvet, lay a clear ball of glass, the size of a large apple. Miranda lifted it out of the box carefully, finding it cool and smooth to her hands, and of a surprising weight.

"This was my grandmother's crystal," said Bella. "She left it to me, along with the cards, when she died— though I've never made much use of it, as my own gift's of a lesser sort. But I'm certain now that the crystal is meant to be yours."

Miranda could not speak, her eyes drawn to the mysterious orb cradled in her palms, so perfectly fashioned that its depths, limpid as water, were nearly indistinguishable from its gleaming surface. It reflected oblique patches of light from the windows, and also, dimly, the curved image of Miranda's face; but otherwise the crystal lay pure and empty, like a vessel waiting to be filled, even while created so full and complete in itself.

"Do you think I'll ever see anything there?" she inquired at last, raising her eyes to Bella's.

"I've no doubt that you will," Bella replied, "but again, it's like the cards. You've got to study the crystal, and come to know it through and through, before you'll understand its powers. We'll begin with it tomorrow, my dear; and though it's best that I keep it here, it's yours, and yours alone, after today."

Miranda gently replaced the crystal upon its bed of velvet and, shutting up the box, returned it to the cupboard. Then she came back and knelt down by the bunk where Bella sat.

"Thank you, Bella, for all you've taught me, and given me," she said humbly. "I'd never have learned anything, if it hadn't been for you. I think you must be the wisest woman on earth, no matter what you may say."

"Nay, child," the old woman said, rising now, and drawing Miranda to her feet. "Nobody's perfect, and we're all of us bound to act foolishly at times. Besides, though I may have taught you a little, it's you must choose your own path in the world, and find how to use your gifts in the best way."

With these words, Bella gave her a parting kiss, and Miranda took her leave, still somewhat overcome by everything that had taken place in a single morning. For the sun had only just risen to noon; and the rest of that day, as well as countless others, lay before her undivulged.

s she walked slowly away from Bella's caravan, Miranda spied Dulcie a short distance off, making for the heath with an empty pail. Quickening her steps, she called out; and Dulcie, turning, greeted her in surprise.

"Why, Miranda," she said, "wherever have you been this morning, and not a bite to eat?"

Miranda laughed. "I forgot about eating," she replied. "I went to look at the sea, and after that I was talking to Bella. It's so much warmer, isn't it? Here, I'll carry that pail."

"Nay, child, there's no need," Dulcie protested; but Miranda simply took the pail from her hand, and they continued over the heath together, Dulcie casting an uncertain glance at her from time to time.

"I've been thinking," Miranda said presently. "There's no reason why I shouldn't keep on with my old work, even while I'm going to Bella for lessons. I know you've wanted to spare me, Dulcie, but I'd take it as a kindness now if you'd let me help as I used to. And I'd like to try my hand at baskets again, if you're willing."

Dulcie stopped and looked at her, disconcerted. "Oh no, dear, that doesn't seem right," she said. "You've got your hands full enough with Bella's cards, and I've seen how weary they leave you. Why, some days you've looked so worn and ill my heart's fairly bled for you."

"Well, it's my own fault if you've been troubled over

me, Dulcie," Miranda said warmly. "I haven't been much of a daughter to you, have I? But now I hope we'll go on as before. I'm not so miserable as I was, and I'll try to behave so you've no cause to fret any longer."

Dulcie's face broke into a smile. "Why, you do seem to be looking happier, Miranda," she exclaimed. "And I don't mind saying I've missed your company. Well, if you're quite sure, it'll be a treat having you work with us again. Besides, Rosa's got a way of disappearing just when more water's wanted."

"Then I'll fetch it myself, after this," said Miranda, striding along towards the spring with such a will that Dulcie was hard pressed to keep pace with her; while after the pail was filled, she carried it homewards with nearly as much ease as when it had been empty.

As they approached the camp, Miranda saw Rosa and Jemmy sitting in the sun on their caravan steps. At the sight of her, Rosa got up and would have retreated inside, had not Miranda called her name—upon which she stopped reluctantly before the door, her face hard and forbidding.

But Miranda walked over to the caravan and, setting down her pail, looked up at Rosa bravely. "I've asked Dulcie if I might try again with the baskets," she said. "And I hope you'll help me, too, Rosa—I'm going to start at the beginning again, and see if I can't do better." She gave Rosa a look of entreaty, hoping that her words would convey more than just the question of baskets.

Rosa regarded her with lifted brows. "Why, I thought you'd got above such things, Miranda," she said coolly, though the fact that she answered at all was a concession of sorts.

"I'm sorry, Rosa," Miranda persisted. "It was all a mistake, only I couldn't see it before. I've still my lessons to do with Bella, but they needn't stand in the way. I've been telling Dulcie that I want us to be just as we were—if you'll forgive me."

"Well, this is a surprise," said Rosa. "I hardly seem to know you today."

"I believe I hardly knew who I was myself," Miranda replied. "But somehow I've finally come to my senses."

Rosa's face softened, and she moved slowly down the steps. "I know I've not been kind to you, Miranda," she said. "I suppose it was chiefly seeing Dulcie so bothered—but there, if you've made your peace with her, we'll try to make it up, too."

She put out her hand; and Miranda clasped it eagerly. "Oh, I *am* glad!" she exclaimed. "If only I'd spoken to both of you sooner—but somehow I couldn't before today. Everything's easier today, it seems. Perhaps I'll even do better with the baskets this time."

Rosa sighed. "Whatever's got into you, I doubt that it's taught you much about basketwork," she said. "Though we'll try again, if you like. I'll start you off, since I hadn't the chance before; and when I'm put out of patience, Dulcie can take another turn."

So leaving them together, Dulcie went off with Jemmy to attend to some washing; while Rosa brought out the rushes, and settled down beside Miranda on the ground.

Yet this afternoon, in the most extraordinary way,

Miranda's fingers seemed to have grown unwontedly skillful—unless it was that the rushes themselves were possessed by some unearthly enchantment. Because from the very first she was able to weave them into flawless circles about their spreading center of rays, until, in mere minutes, the bottom of a basket lay before her, perfectly finished.

Rosa's eyes had widened in disbelief as the work progressed; but now she looked at Miranda with open suspicion. "Here, you've been playing a game with us, haven't you?" she demanded. "You've been practicing in secret—or Bella's been helping you on the sly. Out with it now, what have you been up to?"

"I can't understand it either," Miranda protested, no less astonished than Rosa. "It's all come about without my doing, for I haven't once touched the rushes since that day when Bella told my fortune. I've scarcely even thought about them—you must believe me, Rosa! I wouldn't play you such a trick when we've just made friends again."

"Well, I never saw anything like it," Rosa murmured. "It's as good as I could do myself. What's Bella been teaching you, some sort of magic?"

Miranda did not answer for a moment, wondering at certain thoughts that ran through her head. Then she looked at Rosa with a laugh. "Well, whatever it is, perhaps I'll be less of a nuisance to you after this."

Rosa's face cleared, and she laughed in turn. "That's so," she said. "I shan't complain if you've no more need of my help."

The two of them worked through the afternoon; and

as Rosa showed her the further steps required to curve the sides of the basket upward, and weave in its handle, and finish everything off about the rim, Miranda's fingers seemed only to grow more deft than ever. So that by the time Dulcie was done with her washing and came back to them, one basket was completed, and Miranda had begun the base of a second one.

"Oh dear," said Dulcie, "I see you've had to start over again."

"She's not starting over—she's starting another," Rosa told her. "Just look at this one, if you please!"

"You've never made that basket yourself, Miranda," Dulcie gasped.

Miranda hardly knew how to answer, for fear of sounding too proud; but Rosa took it upon herself to explain.

"Well, it's a wonder, to be sure," Dulcie marveled. "And to think you've done it with nothing to eat all day. There, put these things away now, dear, and rest for a while."

"No, thank you, Dulcie, I'm not in the least tired, and only a little hungry," Miranda said, smiling. "Remember, you're not to make a fuss over me any longer."

"Very well, then, do as you please," Dulcie consented good-humoredly. "Though it's already getting on towards supper." But, to Miranda's continued amazement, so quickly did her fingers fly that by the time the meal was prepared she had finished her second basket, and neatly bundled away the rushes that remained.

As she approached the fire, so much elated by her other triumphs, Miranda even ventured to hope that some way to Leo might also be made plain. But Leo merely gave her a sullen glance, which she dared not challenge; and she could not help feeling a little disheartened.

Nevertheless, it was a comfort to be reconciled with Dulcie and Rosa again; and that night Miranda fell at once into a dreamless sleep, exhausted, after all, by the wonders revealed to her on this long and remarkable day.

ext morning, true to her new resolve, Miranda made herself useful by fetching water, and afterwards helped Dulcie with some additional washing. Then she set to work with the rushes again; but although her skill proved undiminished, her spirits were unaccountably lower than on the previous day.

Rosa and Dulcie worked beside her, talking cheerfully about the weather that held so fine and Tom's plans to break camp in another few weeks. But Miranda, saying little herself, listened with only half an ear. A strange disquiet continued to fret her thoughts—not just her disappointment over Leo, but some further oppression, less readily defined. And when it came time for her lesson with Bella, she was glad to put the rushes aside.

Walking towards Bella's caravan, she saw Nan seated on the steps in conversation with one of the other women; and as Miranda drew near, Nan called out to her, "I hear you've got the better of those baskets at last."

Miranda paused at the foot of the steps, embarrassed. "I must have learned before, but didn't know it," she replied. "It seems so simple now."

Nan's companion smiled. "All's simple to those as know how," she said. "Though you wouldn't have believed my daughter, she was that quick to get the knack of it—and only seven or eight years old at the time. Ah, well, better late than never, isn't it?"

"Now, don't let Maggy put you out," said Nan, seeing

Miranda look even more abashed. "She'll go on about that daughter of hers till you'd like to shake them both!"

Maggy laughed. "There, I didn't mean to belittle you, dear," she said. "And I'll be bound Dulcie's as proud of you as ever I've been of my own girl—even though she did end up running off with a good-for-nothing scamp, and I haven't seen hide nor hair of them since."

"Now then, Miranda, you'd better go along inside," Nan interrupted, laughing herself. "Maggy's apt to tell you her whole life and more if you stop here listening." And she moved aside for Miranda to pass up the steps.

Bella sat waiting for her inside, and bade Miranda shut the door behind her. She, too, had heard about the basketwork. "And how do you think to account for it?" she asked.

"I suppose it's to do with what I saw yesterday," Miranda replied. "But how that's taught me weaving, I can't imagine. It's just that suddenly everything's come right—or nearly everything."

"Ah, yes, you've some riddles left to solve, haven't you?" said Bella sympathetically. "Well, try to set them aside for the present, dear. Just fetch the crystal, and we'll begin with it straightaway."

Miranda went to the cupboard and took the box down from its shelf. Still she felt an inexplicable agitation; and when the crystal was set out before her, and Bella instructed her to gaze into its depths and think of nothing else, she found that her mind wandered away to Leo, and the baskets, and even to what the woman Maggy had been saying.

Shaking her head impatiently, she attempted to drive away these thoughts. But for some reason the crystal appeared less magical today, as if it were, in truth, nothing more than a ball of polished glass. Indeed, Miranda felt she might as well have sat gazing on the homeliest of objects—an apple, an onion, an ordinary cobblestone—for all she could make of this emptily glittering bauble.

Sensing her vexation, Bella counseled her to stop and rest. She herself got up and went to the door. "I'll leave you alone for a bit," she said. "Try again presently; but remember, you needn't expect to see anything at first— or for many a day, as it may be."

After Bella was gone, Miranda sighed, and trained her eyes again on the inscrutable globe. But although she succeeded to some extent in routing her earlier thoughts, the persistent shadow upon her mind would not be dispelled. The more she sought to concentrate, the more oppressive it grew, until the crystal itself seemed dulled and darkened, as if her own uneasiness had overspread it like an obscuring cloud.

She looked away at last, and rubbed her eyes. Once again the crystal lay icily clear. Yet now its very clarity appeared to mock her with unfathomable secrets, much as the sea had done the day before—except that the sea had also laughed in generous celebration, whereas the crystal's mockery was unrelenting, and even vaguely sinister.

Miranda shivered, and could scarcely bear to look at it further. However, when, against her will, she did so, she noticed an alteration in the crystal's appearance, almost as if it stirred a little, shrugging away the bounds of its glassy skin. Then, slowly, its shining surface seemed to dissolve, so that her gaze sank straight to the crystal's core: no longer a transparent substance but an absence, an inward hollow that opened before her like a black abyss, its vacancy as profound as the fullness of light she had beheld in the sea.

Appalled by this spectacle, Miranda would have drawn back from it—except that now it seemed to lie everywhere about her, while she herself had lost the power to move. And at the same time there arose at the center of that darkness a ghostly illumination, like a morbid phosphorescence, or the chill, deceptive light of the moon, waxing steadily more and more distinct until it had assumed a fully articulate shape. And as she recognized that shape, Miranda felt the blood stand frozen in her veins.

She saw it to be the image of Death, the very Death of her cards, a figure of barren bones, its face a grinning skull—but a figure far more terrifying than any picture, for its jaws gaped and chattered in silent glee, while it proceeded to dance a horribly sprightly jig over the ground of the dark.

Its insidious capering circled ever nearer to Miranda, until Death danced before her, one bony hand extended, as though inviting her to join in the same dance herself. There was, moreover, something familiar in that hand: and she perceived all at once that its gaunt, white fingers were her father's, the way they had always looked to her in the past, so pale and clever and cold.

Gazing in terror again upon Death's face, she saw

that it, too, was changed to her father's, wan and wasted as a skull—though wearing a grin no longer, but instead an expression of anguish. For now that meager hand was outstretched to her not in sly bidding but in desperate supplication: no longer Death's hand, but that of Death's prisoner, entreating Miranda's pity, and even her aid.

She would have cried out; but the next moment this apparition was withdrawn from her sight and resolved into the blackness whence it had risen; from which there seemed no escape, neither for that wretched prisoner nor for Miranda herself. Once more she sought in vain to break free. Then, even as she despaired, a faint sound reached her ears, like a voice, or merely the echo of a voice, calling her name—not her familiar name but her new one, Mira, sprung from an indeterminate source, remote beyond definition.

It crossed the embracing void like a fine, luminous beam; and she found that she could move slowly along its path, towards another place where the darkness was thinned, and that vibrant beacon summoned her ever more clearly; until, with a final effort, she emerged into daylight—the daylight of Bella's caravan, where Miranda sat as before, gazing upon the crystal, although it was again shrunk small and glossy and impenetrable.

Then she heard another voice, close by, speaking her name, *Miranda!* and found Bella standing over her, an anxious look on her face.

"Oh, Bella," she said in a frightened whisper. "I've seen such dreadful things!"

"There, I expect I shouldn't have left you alone," Bella exclaimed. "What was it you saw, my child?"

"The crystal went all dark," Miranda answered unsteadily, "and I seemed to have fallen into it, and couldn't get out. And then I saw Death, the one in my cards, only this was much worse; and in the end it changed into my father, as if he was dead himself. Oh, Bella, I thought I'd never get away—except I heard someone calling me, and it brought me back at last."

Bella looked very grave. "I'd never have thought you'd see any such thing, straight off," she said. "And yet I might have—I knew from the first you were troubled today. Yes, I'm afraid it was wrong of me, for the crystal's not the same as the cards. They've got a voice of their own, but the crystal speaks more of what's in your mind; and if you've thoughts you haven't made your peace with, they can appear very dark indeed."

Miranda found little consolation in these words. "But was it truly my father?" she asked. "Do you think he could be dying, or even dead, without my knowing it?"

"Nay, it's not for me to say," Bella replied slowly. "It belongs to your own sight, even if it's not made altogether clear to you. Though it's true, your father was there in the cards, with some misfortune upon him."

"Oh, Bella, whatever am I to do?" Miranda quavered. "I feel so strange, as if I hadn't yet escaped from that awful place."

"I think you ought to go and rest," Bella said gently. "A good deal's been asked of you these past two days;

it's seeing so much at once that's tried your strength. Come and visit me tonight, and we'll see how you are by then."

Still shaken, Miranda returned to her own caravan, passing by Dulcie and Rosa with only a nod. She lay down on Dulcie's bunk and shut her eyes, but as soon as she did so, a rush of darkness threatened to engulf her once more, and even when she opened them, its menacing presence remained. After a time, unable to lie still any longer, she got up and went outside again. Then, trusting herself to speak to no one at present, she walked away to the heath.

But the joyous mirth she had seen reflected there the day before was fled; while now in its place lurked only the wintry laughter of the dark, blighting the budded spring at its very source, and dooming even the full-blown flowers of summer to dust. For it seemed that at last Miranda saw the greatest joke of all, the joke which made a mockery of every other laughter—even the paradisal laughter of light, whose radiance was revealed to be nothing but fool's gold, a glittering counterfeit, a brilliant, worthless dross.

Death's laughter proved the Fool himself just that, a blind and innocent dupe, whose merry capering must pitch him headlong into the dark abyss before him. But worse by far, Death had made a fool of Miranda. For while that figure in the crystal had put on her father's face, she understood now that it could just as easily have worn her own.

What was her face at this moment but a flimsy veil,

masking her own sly skull? Nor did it make any difference whether her skin was fair, or grayed with ashes, or stained a gypsy brown: all were merely fleeting disguises flung over that truth of bone.

Yet, even while she stood transfixed by this terrible revelation, the heath about her lay calm in the late-afternoon sun, unmindful of the similar fate concealed at its roots. And in the midst of her horror Miranda was struck with pity for those infant leaves and blooms in their innocent growth, as they played out their hopeful parts in the hopeless tragedy of the world.

Though even more deeply, Miranda pitied herself. For over all that heath, she alone perceived the destiny none could escape; she alone was delivered from foolish ignorance, and condemned to a foresight worse than any blindness. In fact, she wondered how she was to go on living from day to day, forever aware of the chasm agape at her feet—while still beset by her own persistent hopes and longings, vain though she knew them to be.

Both foolish and wise at once, she thought, as Bella's words came back to her. Yet these words meant nothing to her now but a further folly; and at last, with a shrug of despair, she turned, and took her way slowly back to the camp.

y the time she got there, the gypsies were gathering for their supper, both Nan and Bella among the others that evening; and afterwards Nan urged Tom to bring out his fiddle again—to which, this time, he consented willingly, in honor of the springlike weather.

Miranda had eaten in silence, feeling Dulcie's eyes upon her, but unable to summon up more than a weak smile in return. Even the genial fire afforded her no comfort tonight. Its dancing flames only seemed to her tarnished by the ashes to which they must fall, or even tainted with some base and treacherous nature of their own, ready at any moment to turn on these gypsies who trusted in them for warmth and light—the way those other three had perished in their fiery caravan not so many years before, or as Nan, though living on, remained at the mercy of the fever smoldering in her blood, playing its stealthy game with her day by day, until it might choose to flare up and consume her altogether.

So that when Tom opened up his black fiddle case—which now, to Miranda's lugubrious fancy, resembled nothing so much as a dismal coffin—and lifted out the gleaming fiddle from within, Miranda could have wept at the sight of it: so brave and so frail it appeared, so useless a weapon to be wielded against the infinite sway of the night.

Yet, as Tom began to play, and the fiddle's music filled her ears once more with its intimations of joy and sorrow, celebration and mourning, inextricably wedded and woven together, there slowly dawned on Miranda the sense that it held some further meaning as well, almost as if that music sang to her of her own plight, and sought to relieve her own despair.

She listened more intently, gazing on Tom's rough, brown face as he swept the bow back and forth over the strings; as though Tom himself, standing there strong and alive in his threadbare clothing, might somehow deliver her from the darkness into whose power she had fallen. As though, even while Tom stood with his feet set firmly on the ground, his fiddle played the tune to a dance as bold as Death's: a dance that was danced at the very brink of the grave, but whose steps were no more deceived than they were daunted.

And it came to her all in a flash that Tom's music was not only bold but wise. Tom was no fool, blind to the perilous shadows yawning about that firelit circle; nor had Death outwitted any of these other gypsies, who danced in spirit tonight as gaily as ever, and only cherished their dancing the more because they knew it must come to an end. Only too well they knew it: but it was in that very knowledge, and by way of their reckless merriment, that they challenged the gleeful dark, flouting Death's immutable grin with their mortal laughter.

Then perhaps, by the same token, the Fool himself was not blind, but trod his own blithe measure in defiant mockery of Death. Perhaps the Fool had the last laugh after all, and his laughter, too, was there in Tom's music —a laughter sprung out of wisdom, not folly, acknowledging the infernal chasms of darkness as well as the celestial realms of light. For now, as she listened entranced, Miranda began to hear another sound in that music, intricately threaded through the rest—as if Tom's fiddle were singing the sound of her own name. *Mira*, the music sang to her, *Mira*; and a voice within her echoed that name in recognition, and joyful reply.

As if for the first time she had claimed that subtle identity: Mira, the name of her own hidden truth; Mira, whose wisdom arose from the inmost matters of heart and mind, matters wrought deeper than any bone; Mira, whose starry image sprang from those depths unquelled, to match its fires against the obscuring dark. And Miranda sat rapt, singing that wonderful name over and over in her head, until her voice became another part of Tom's music, and her spirit danced as valiantly as his, and the Fool's, and the others'.

Even when, at length, Tom drew the bow down over the strings in an ultimate flourish and lowered his fiddle again, some reverberation of its music sang on in Miranda's ears, with that *Mira, Mira*, constant still—an echo immortal as wisdom itself, whose radiance was reflected from life to life, from age to age, forever eluding the grasp of single-minded Death; as even mortal life was thus preserved, borne on in its own ceaseless echoes and reflections: its original breathing spark still caught at the quick of every ephemeral flower or flesh, thrown forth again and again to sow the dust with vigorous light, and raise up new generations, charged with the same imperishable gold.

And it was then that Miranda discovered the answer for which she had seemed to be searching throughout that day—though she saw, too, that it had lain all the while at the root of her troubled thoughts. It was an answer at once simple and incontestable. She must go, as that deathly vision of her father, as the cards themselves, had so plainly directed her, back to the life she had fled. She must keep faith with the sources of her own flesh and blood, by returning to the parents she had denied: to remedy whatever ills might have befallen them, and so to make amends.

Ennobled with Mira's gifts and powers she might be; but it was clear to her now that she should never prove worthy of them, nor yet be free to perfect them, until she had dealt wisely and bravely with Miranda's humbler affairs. And somehow her final acceptance of this difficult course dispersed the last traces of darkness from her mind, almost as though the sun had blazed forth in the middle of the night to light the path before her.

She rose to her feet without hesitation; and having given her thanks to Tom, hastened away to seek out Bella, who had already taken Nan back to their caravan. Nan was in bed, but not asleep, and Miranda spoke to her first. "I'm so glad you asked Tom to play again," she said. "I think he played better than ever tonight."

Nan smiled. "Well, you've really Mother to thank," she confessed. "She thought of it even before I did—though of course it always does me a world of good to hear Tom's music."

Miranda looked at Bella, who said, regarding her acutely, "It's done you good yourself, if I'm not mistaken."

Miranda laughed. "You knew what I'd hear if Tom played, didn't you?" she exclaimed. "And you were right, I've got over all that I saw today. But I've seen something else besides, and found what I must do."

Bella's face grew sober. "I'm almost sorry to hear you say so, Miranda. There's none of us wish you to go away."

Miranda stared at her. "However did you know?" she marveled.

"It was there in your cards, wasn't it?" Bella replied. "And today's only brought it to its proper time."

"What's this?" Nan inquired anxiously, sitting up again. "Surely you're not thinking of leaving us, Miranda?"

Miranda sat down beside her. "I've got to go home, Nan," she said quietly. "There are matters left unsettled there, and I can't be free until I've put them right."

Nan's sunken eyes filled with tears. "I'd hoped you were to stay with us always," she murmured. "You've come to be one of us, despite Tom's doubts." But the next moment she smiled again, and patted Miranda's hand. "Don't listen to me, dear," she apologized. "I've got a bit tired with being out of bed. No, if it's meant for you to go, we certainly mustn't keep you."

Then they heard footsteps outside, and Tom and Leo came in, both appearing much surprised to find Miranda there; but Bella spoke up at once.

"Miranda's just come to say she'll be leaving," she told

them. "She feels there's trouble at home, and she's made up her mind to go."

Tom looked at Miranda in astonishment. "Going home?" he said. "When you've been so dead set on staying?"

Miranda answered him steadily. "It's not that I want to, Tom," she said, with a quick glance at Leo, who stood with lowered eyes, a little apart. "Only I've seen that I must."

Tom studied her appraisingly. "So you'd leave us after all," he said, "and everything Bella's been teaching you? Well, my girl, there's more to you than I thought—and I'll give you my hand on it." He put out his hard brown hand and clasped Miranda's warmly. "And if ever you see fit to come back to us, you'll be welcome, in spite of anything I may have said before."

"Thank you, Tom," Miranda replied. "I only hope I'll be able to find you when I'm free."

Tom gave her a grin. "You may depend on Bella for that," he said. "She'll be sure to see the workings of it, and then I'll not know a moment's peace until we've come to fetch you again."

Miranda stole another glance at Leo, but he only continued gazing at the floor. So she sighed and turned away to leave; but then stopped short. "Why, I haven't thought of how I'm to get home," she exclaimed. "I don't even know the way."

Tom rubbed his chin, perplexed. "It's not so easy, that's true," he agreed. "You can't walk all that distance by yourself, and we'll be moving north when we go on, quite out of your direction."

Leo raised his head. "I'll take her," he said. "We can ride on Dolly, she's steadiest out of the shafts; and it won't take so long if we keep to the highroads."

The others stared at Leo, amazed—except for Bella, who nodded approvingly. But Miranda could scarcely believe her ears, nor yet her eyes; for Leo smiled at her now, as though no trouble had ever stood between them.

Nan was the first to recover her speech. "Well, Leo, I call that a handsome offer," she said. "I thought nothing in the world could take you away from that dog and your rabbiting! We've hardly seen you at all this winter—and nothing to say for yourself when you have come home."

Leo looked distinctly chagrined. "Never mind about that," he muttered. "It wasn't the rabbits kept me away."

"That'll do very well," Bella pronounced. "Leo will see you safely home, Miranda, you may be sure."

"I thank you, Leo, it's very kind of you," Miranda said faintly. "When do you think to go?"

"I suppose tomorrow's as good a time as any," Leo replied. "The sooner you're off, the sooner you'll be coming back." But although his words were spoken lightly, his eyes, as they met Miranda's, held a new sorrow of their own.

"Then I'll be ready in the morning," Miranda said. "But I'd better go now and tell Dulcie—though I don't like doing so."

"I'll come out with you," said Leo, and followed her through the door. They walked towards Dulcie's caravan in a constrained silence; but at the foot of its steps he put a hand on Miranda's arm.

"Before we're away tomorrow, I've something to say to you," he began in a low voice. "It seems I've been a proper fool"—and he laughed abruptly. "I had the Fool in my cards when Bella read them; perhaps this is what it was about. But whatever it was," he continued, "I've been mistaken. You see, when Bella told us you were going to learn the cards and such, I thought you'd been set above me. I thought you'd have no use for me any longer, and I'd only stand in your way."

Though Miranda would have spoken, he went on quickly. "But then, when I saw tonight you'd give it all up, just to help the very folk you ran off from, it seemed those other things couldn't really be so much to you—at least, not enough to keep us apart." And now he stopped, at a loss for words, though he still held fast to her arm.

"Oh, Leo, you were a silly goose," Miranda said, "but so was I, to let you go on thinking such things. I've been miserable over you for so long—but now it's set right, at last."

"Nay, I don't know that it is," Leo objected. "For what if you don't come back? What if you make up your mind to stop there, once you're home again?"

"And what if I do come back?" Miranda said softly. "What then, Leo?"

"Don't pretend you don't know what I'm saying," he chided her. "I'd have spoken of it before, only this other matter got in the way. If you come back, and if you like, we'll marry. There, I've asked you straight out; though of course it's for you to answer as you please."

Miranda was silent a moment, unable to speak. Then she lifted her head, and kissed him. "I'll come back to you, Leo," she said gravely, "and it's not just myself saying it, but the cards. Your own card was there, when Bella read mine—the Knave of Wands, there at the end of my trials."

At this, Leo put his arms about her, and kissed her in return. "That's settled, then," he said. "For the cards won't change, and no more will I. But there, you'd better go in now, as we'll be starting off early tomorrow."

Thus he left her, and Miranda went inside with a full heart. Rosa and Jemmy were already abed, but Dulcie, waiting up, greeted her with something of her old anxiety; and only looked the more disquieted when Miranda said she must speak to her.

"I've two things to tell you, Dulcie," she began. "One you may not like, I'm afraid, though the other one's better—at least, I hope you'll think so. But the first is that I've seen I must go home to my parents for a time."

Dulcie caught her breath, and briefly shut her eyes. Then she gave a sigh of resignation. "Well, dear, I've always thought it must come to this," she said. "Didn't I tell you myself you'd a bounden duty to your mother? Not that it doesn't grieve me to part with you—but I've had a share in you, and I see as it's her turn now. Though I hope you'll be coming to us again one day?" she added wistfully.

"I'm sure to, Dulcie," Miranda replied. "It was in my cards, that all would end happily; and besides, there's something more—it's myself and Leo, you see. He's taking me home tomorrow, on one of the horses; and later, when everything's made right, I'm to marry him, if you're willing."

Dulcie's face broke into a smile. "Willing, Miranda dear? Why, it's the very thing I'd hoped for—only Leo's been so downhearted these past months, I'd feared it had come to naught between you. Ah, this does make me happy! For then you'll be my true daughter at last."

Now Rosa raised her head from the bunk where she had appeared to be fast asleep. "Don't think I haven't been listening to every word," she told them. "And I must confess, Miranda, I'm sorry to see you go."

"I'm sorry to leave you, too, Rosa," Miranda replied. "But I hope you won't mind having me for your niece, if I'm to marry Leo someday."

"I expect I'll be just as bad-tempered, as your aunt," Rosa said, with a laugh. "But I'll be that glad to see Leo happily settled down—he's moped about on his own quite long enough."

Miranda and Dulcie laughed, as well; and at last they prepared for bed. After the candles were put out, however, Rosa spoke up again. "Don't forget to take that coin from Jemmy," she said. "You'll have need of it now; and he's got your handkerchief, besides."

"No, Rosa, let him keep them for me," Miranda answered. "Then they'll be another sign that I'm coming back."

"Just as you like," Rosa said sleepily. "Though I can't promise he won't lose them."

Then the darkened caravan fell silent, except for the distant sound of the sea: whose abiding harmony sang in Miranda's ears, until, in spite of her own mingled joys and sorrows, she was soothed away to sleep.

ulcie was up even before Miranda next morning, preparing a parcel of food for the travelers to carry with them. Rosa herself, while rising later, pressed a sixpence for the journey into Miranda's hand; and when she went out to take her leave of the other gypsies, each had something to offer her, whether a bit of food wrapped up, a penny or two, or some small but well-intended keepsake.

She went last to Bella's caravan, where she found Nan not so strong as the day before, but sitting up to bid Miranda farewell, and to present her with a little silver brooch of her own. Miranda fastened it over her heart, thanking Nan with a kiss, and a few tears she could not check; yet Nan herself was calm and cheerful, and said she was certain to be in better health by the time they met again.

Miranda then turned to Bella and embraced her. The old woman's eyes shone bright, though not with tears; and drawing Miranda over to the cupboard, she took out a small packet tied up in a red silk cloth.

"The crystal must wait for you here," she said, "but these are yours to take with you."

"Bella, not your cards," gasped Miranda. "Oh no, you mustn't give them up."

"Nay, they're passed on to you, now, as they were to me," Bella insisted. "They'll serve you better when they're your own. Look after them well, and they'll guide you when I'm not able to myself."

Miranda felt a strange chill at these words. But Bella, kissing her quickly, led her to the door and, with a last smile, turned away; and Miranda saw her no more.

Leo waited before Dulcie's caravan holding the chestnut mare, over whose stout back a blanket was fastened, with another rolled up and tied across her withers. Dulcie stood with Tom and several others nearby, a basket in her hand; and now, smiling bravely, she said that there was food enough in the basket for a day or so, and that Miranda's former clothes were also packed up inside.

Miranda thanked her; but after a moment's thought looked through the basket and took out her shawl, never worn since that night when she had changed it for Dulcie's. "I want you to keep this, Dulcie," she said, putting the shawl into her hands. "I've had yours all this time, it's only right."

Dulcie looked troubled. "Nay, but it's too fine," she said. "That other's all patches, and you'll want your own at home."

"No, I shan't; or I'll find one there," Miranda persisted. "And for that matter, Rosa must have my old skirt"—and she looked about. "Where's she got to, then?"

Dulcie smiled sadly. "She told me to say goodbye for her," she said. "It seems she couldn't face seeing you off herself. Rosa's got a soft heart, you know, for those she's fond of."

Miranda felt the tears spring to her eyes. "Take her

the skirt, then," she said, and threw her arms about Dulcie in a parting embrace.

Leo, gathering up the reins, jumped astride the mare; while Tom, who had stood by quietly until now, lifted Miranda and set her on behind him. "Mind you look after her, Leo," he said. "And you, missy, see you come back before too long—as I hear there's to be a wedding when you do, and I'll be keeping my fiddle in tune for the occasion."

Then, giving the mare's flank a sturdy slap, he turned and walked away. The mare moved forward abruptly, and Miranda had all she could do to keep her seat, with Dulcie's basket on one arm, and the other tight about Leo's waist. But as they rode off, with Bruno's excited barks and the gypsies' cries of farewell in their ears, Miranda saw Tom turn again to watch them; and he remained standing so until they had gone some distance across the heath.

Despite Miranda's pleasure in Leo's presence, their way was not an easy one. The weather had reverted to chilly clouds, the mare's back was far from comfortable, and Miranda's every bone seemed to be aching before they had reached the main road. Both riders fell silent, neither one of them so hopeful as on the previous night. Miranda even began to wonder whether she had made the right decision. It seemed very hard to be leaving behind those who were dearest to her, for the sake of others who might not entirely welcome her return; and Leo's company on this journey could only make their parting more difficult in the end.

But there was no going back now; and when they left

the road that evening, and ate their supper in the shelter of a lonely hedgerow, at least Miranda's bodily aches were eased, and she began to feel somewhat less disconsolate.

Leo did his best to cheer her further, telling her of the gypsies' travels in the past, and about his own boyhood, when his father had taken him hunting for rabbits, and taught him how to clean and skin them as well. "Though I came near to skinning myself at the start," he said with a laugh, showing Miranda a pale scar that ran the length of his thumb.

"Why, Leo," she exclaimed, tracing it over with her finger. "I'd never noticed it before. Though I remember watching your hands that day when you helped me with the sticks. Yes, I'd begun to love you even then," she mused, smoothing his callused palm. "I wonder if it's here in your hand—that day, and everything that's happened since?"

Bending her head impulsively, she kissed his palm, afterwards closing the fingers up tight. "Now that kiss will always be a part of your fortune," she said, smiling at last, "no matter what else is there."

Leo put his arm about her and drew her close. "Don't let's talk of fortunes," he said in a low voice. "I'd sooner forget what's to come, and only think of us now."

They sat quietly thus for a time; but then Leo sighed and, kissing Miranda gently, got to his feet. "Remember, Tom told me to look after you," he said, "and there's a long road ahead tomorrow. You'll have need of your rest."

So together they made a bed of dry leaves beneath the hedge and, wrapped in their blankets, lay down to sleep. And for the moment Miranda felt it was worth every trial that might await her at home, to be here with the sweet, musty smell of leaves in her nostrils, and the night wind on her cheek, and Leo so close beside her that she could hear the whisper of his breathing.

Next day the weather was clear, but colder still. They went on at a good pace, stopping only once in a village to buy more bread. Passersby stared at them inquisitively, and one or two were heard to remark on the free and easy ways of gypsies. But Leo took no notice, and Miranda only pulled the kerchief down closer over her hair and made sure of Bella's gold hoops at her ears, prouder than ever to be wearing them.

Otherwise, nobody paid them much heed. They stopped that night as before, and ate their cold supper in a peaceful kind of melancholy. Yet they spoke less and less as with every hour their time together waned, almost as though they had already parted and only the wraiths of themselves were left to pursue the rest of that journey together.

Late on the third day, the lands about them grew hilly and more heavily wooded. Recognizing in their changed aspect the look of her own countryside, Miranda tightened her arm about Leo's waist; and before very long, when the road ascended to the top of a final rise, they saw spread out in the distance below them a mottled sea of roofs and towers, faintly gilded by the last rays of the sun.

Leo reined in, and they both contemplated this unhappy prospect.

"Somehow I thought we'd never come to it," Miranda sighed. "It doesn't seem that it could have waited there all the while I've been away."

"It's there, right enough," Leo said glumly. "Though I'd sooner not have set eyes on it again." But he urged the mare forward, and they descended the long slope. At the bottom, Leo drew up once more. "I'd better set you down here," he said. "It's not far to walk now, and it wouldn't do for me to be seen with you in the town."

Miranda could not bring herself to speak. But Leo slid from the mare's back, lifted Miranda down in turn, and for a moment they clung to one another in silent misery.

Then, with tears in her eyes, Miranda bent her head and began rummaging through Dulcie's basket. "Here's the last of the bread," she said, "and you'd better take this sixpence Rosa gave me. No, don't make a fuss over it—if I'm to be your wife, I've a say in such matters." And smiling despite her tears, she pressed the coin into his hand.

Leo smiled briefly, too; and now he drew from his pocket a small parcel. "On that subject, I've something for you myself," he said. "Though it's from Mother as well."

Miranda undid the paper and found inside a gold ring, set with a single garnet. "It belonged to my sister, who died," Leo said quietly. "But Mother said it could serve as a token between us."

The ring was more of a size to fit a child; but Miranda slipped it on her little finger, and held out her hand for Leo to see. "I'll wear it always, Leo," she said. "It'll be a comfort while we're apart; and perhaps it'll bring us together again, besides."

"Nay, don't say perhaps," Leo said uneasily, his face darker than ever. "There, you'd better be off, before I make a fool of myself here in the road."

"Well, I've already made one of myself," said Miranda, drying her eyes with the back of her hand. "Still, we're neither of us such fools as we were—we know we're bound to each other, and that's more than enough wisdom to go on with, isn't it?"

With these words she kissed him lightly and walked quickly away towards the town.

er noble words notwithstanding, Miranda felt thoroughly desolate as she made her way along, remembering the night so many months ago when she had followed that same road in the opposite direction. Nor, as she entered the town and retraced her steps along its twilit streets, could she help imagining that they led her into some doleful prison, one from which she might never walk away free, no matter what the cards had foretold.

The market square this evening was nearly deserted, although, as she passed the spot where the gypsies' barrow had stood, she could almost glimpse their phantom figures; yet the next instant they were fled, and only the barren cobblestones lay before her, mournful and gray in the chill dusk.

Leaving the square behind, she soon turned into her own street and came in sight of the apothecary's shop, smaller than she had remembered it, but otherwise unchanged. She hesitated before the door, as the shop was already darkened and locked for the night, and even now she was uncertain of how she ought to greet her parents. But at last she pulled the handle of the bell, and stood back to await whatever might follow.

After a space she heard footsteps approaching, and the bolts withdrawn. It was, however, neither of her parents who opened the door, but her aunt, whose son had been made the apothecary's apprentice. Holding up a candle, she looked out cautiously and, seeing Miranda on the doorstep, drew back and shut the door halfway. "Get along with you," she said sharply. "We've nothing to give you, and we don't want any brooms or clothes pegs if you've come selling them."

"Stay, Aunt, it's Miranda!" she cried.

The woman put out her head once more. "What's that you say about Miranda?" she asked warily.

"It's me, Aunt," Miranda persisted. "I've come home again." Realizing how strange a figure she must appear, she moved closer to the light and pulled off the kerchief that covered her hair.

"Mercy on us," gasped her aunt. "It's never Miranda, in those disgraceful gypsy rags! And what on earth have you done to your face? Come inside, my girl—though I can scarcely believe it, even now."

Miranda entered the shop, which looked to her gloomier than ever in the light of her aunt's candle, its flame reflected dimly in the glassware ranged upon the counter. "I'd better go straight up to Mother and Father," she said, moving towards the stairs.

Her aunt put out a hand and stopped her. "They're not here," she said, an odd expression on her face. "I see you've not heard."

"I've heard nothing," said Miranda, her heart sinking. "I've been far away all winter. What is it, Aunt?"

"Your father died some weeks ago, I'm sorry to say," her aunt replied, her voice cold and reproving.

"Oh no, Aunt," Miranda breathed, aghast. "It's the

very worst thing I feared! I sensed something was wrong, and that's why I came back."

"Well, you've come too late," her aunt said grimly. "Not much good, is it, remembering your parents just when it suits you? Though I daresay you may be some help to your mother, as she'll take none from me. Went right off and found herself lodgings, she did, as soon as James and I came to live here ourselves. You do know your father arranged to leave everything to James—quite like a son to him, James had become. But your mother feels she's been done out of her own property, and she won't hear of stopping with us, even though she'd have a room to herself upstairs."

"But where is she living?" asked Miranda, now doubly distressed.

"Only round the corner, in Gate Street," her aunt replied uneasily. "Not a very nice place, I'm afraid; there wasn't much money left, you see, apart from what belonged to the shop. She'd be taken care of, if she'd come back to us, but there's been no reasoning with the woman; in fact, she's been most peculiar lately when I've tried to visit her. Of course, she's always had a mind of her own, your mother—the same as some others I could mention."

Miranda made no reply, but her face grew hot with a mixture of shame and sorrow and indignation.

Her aunt continued to eye her sternly. "I can't think what you meant by leaving home that way," she said. "At first they said you were stolen by the gypsies, though I never believed it myself. 'She's run off out of sheer contrariness,' I said. 'It'll serve her right if she comes to grief.' And your father agreed—though I must say he was never himself after you'd gone."

Miranda, entirely daunted, turned away to the door. "I must go and find Mother," she said in a faint voice. "Which house is it?"

"Number twenty," her aunt replied, with a deprecating sniff.

"Good night, then, Aunt," Miranda said. "I'm sorry for all that's happened. Though I suppose it's not much use my saying so now."

"A bit tardy, my girl," her aunt observed dryly. "But we'll not shirk our own duty to your mother, if you can get her to change her mind. And I expect we can find room for yourself as well, if you're here to stay. Blood's thicker than water, and nobody can say we've turned away our kin."

"Thank you, Aunt," Miranda said wearily. "I'll try to do what's best." And she departed, shutting the door behind her.

It was dark by now, and the narrow street into which she soon turned was poorly lit. But after some searching, she found the number marked on a dilapidated pillar, and mounted the steps. She rang twice before there came any answer; but at length the door was opened by a hunched old woman in a dressing gown and carpet slippers, who peered out at her suspiciously. "Who did you want, then?" she demanded.

Miranda was obliged to repeat her mother's name twice before the woman made it out. "Top floor, the door on your left," she informed her grudgingly; and with a contemptuous glance at Miranda's attire, shuffled back to her own quarters.

Miranda ascended two flights, and found herself in a cramped little hallway. Turning to the left, she tapped at the door; but although she heard some movement within, no one appeared. So she knocked more loudly, until the door was opened a crack, and a voice said, "It's no use coming any longer, I won't see you."

"No, Mother, it's your daughter, Miranda," she said urgently.

"Ah, it's a dream, then," her mother's voice murmured, and the door was shut again.

Miranda continued to knock. "Truly, it's Miranda—do let me in," she begged; and at last her mother allowed the door to swing wide.

"I thought you were dead," she said in a hoarse whisper. "Or are you come back as a ghost?"

"No, Mother, I'm quite alive," Miranda said, moving inside. "Come over by the light, and you'll see."

A candle flickered on the table at the center of the room, where a single chair was set; but aside from a low bed and a chest of drawers, the room contained no other furniture, and its plastering was cracked and water-stained. No fire burned in the grate, nor did it appear that one had been laid there for some time.

Appalled by these surroundings, Miranda turned to regard her mother. She was dressed in a black velvet gown, a handsome garment once, though at present much the worse for wear. Red locks heavily streaked with gray fell disheveled to her shoulders, framing a face grown pale and haggard; and the hand she put out to touch Miranda's own red hair was as wrinkled as an old woman's.

"No, there's no mistaking that hair," her mother said, with a faint smile. "But you seem to be got up as a gypsy —did they really carry you off, then?"

"I'll tell you about it presently," Miranda answered her, "but first we must talk about yourself. For you don't look at all well, Mother, and I wonder you can stop in such an unhealthy place when Aunt says there's a room set aside for you at home."

Her mother's face darkened. "And well she may say so, seeing as she and that son of hers have stolen the roof from over my head! You see, dear," she said, lowering her voice, "I'm sure your father never meant James to have the rest of the house, along with the shop, while I was alive. But taken ill so suddenly as he was, he'd no chance to speak of it, and it wasn't made plain in his will.

"Besides, your aunt's always been a schemer," she went on, looking about her in a queer, furtive manner. "I believe she plotted it from the start, the minute she'd got her foot in the door with James made apprentice. The way she kept hinting, after you'd gone, that we'd as much as driven you out—so that your father lost heart, and died when he'd only been ill of a few days' fever.

"And now, of course, she wants me back," Miranda's mother whispered, "where she can keep an eye on me, and I won't go talking of her to others. Besides, I've one or two bits of jewelry she'd like to get hold of. Oh yes, if I went back now she'd see to it that I was soon dead myself—and she'd have the ring off my finger, and the chain from my neck, as soon as I'd drawn my final breath."

Miranda had listened to this recital in growing horror. "Oh no, Mother, you must be mistaken," she exclaimed. "Aunt may be selfish, but I'm sure she'd never be so wicked as all that."

"No, she's a sly, clever woman, Miranda," her mother insisted, her eyes still darting about the room, "and I won't set foot in that house while she's there. You mustn't either," she added, anxiously grasping Miranda's arm. "She's a danger to both of us now!"

"All right then, Mother," Miranda replied soothingly, "we'll both stop here, at least until you're better. You can't be well, or you wouldn't have got such dreadful notions into your head. Come along, I'll see you to bed, and tomorrow I'll go out and get some wood for a fire— this room's as cold as ice, it's no wonder you're ill."

Indeed, having persuaded her mother into bed, and afterwards searching about the room, Miranda found neither firewood nor food, only a little water in a chipped jug on the mantelshelf, along with some dusty crockery and cooking utensils. She sat down helplessly at the table, her eyes fixed unseeing on the candle flame, wondering whatever she was to do. For in her worst anticipations she had never thought to find matters so bleak as this, nor could she help blaming herself for the whole affair.

If only she had remained at home, perhaps her father might not have died, nor her aunt pushed her way into the house so easily. Or if at the very start she had learned the work of the shop, her cousin James should never have been apprenticed, nor made her father's heir. Overcome with self-reproach, Miranda laid her head on her arms and wept.

But after a time, past weeping any longer, she blew out the candle and went to lie down in the space at her mother's side. Nevertheless, her troubled thoughts persisted; and exhausted though she was, it was some time before they allowed her to sink into a fitful doze.

iranda awoke cold and stiff next morning, to find her mother still asleep and the wan light of dawn creeping in through the window. Sighing, she got out of bed; and after a brief attempt to smooth her hair before a tarnished mirror propped up on the chest, she began searching through Dulcie's basket for the few pennies given her by the gypsies.

But presently her mother, opening her eyes and seeing what Miranda was about, told her to look beneath a corner of the mattress, where she found hidden a small purse containing several silver coins and one or two coppers.

"That's all I've got left," her mother said drearily. "I came away with nothing else but what I was wearing."

"How ever did you expect to manage on so little?" Miranda protested.

"Ah, well, I've not had much appetite," her mother replied, "and the old woman can wait for her rent. Besides, there's my ring and my chain, and I'd rather sell them off than let your aunt get hold of them." Her eyes grew restless and fearful again. "I'd have made the money last a while," she added, "only now you've come, you'd better buy in something to eat for yourself."

First, however, Miranda fetched a jugful of water from the tap downstairs and, bathing her mother's face and hands, settled her more comfortably in bed. Then, taking

Dulcie's basket and her mother's purse, she went out into the street.

Few people were yet abroad, but coming upon a little shop already open, she bought a loaf of bread, some eggs, and an ounce of tea; and after searching along another street, she discovered a builder's yard where she was able to obtain a bundle of scrap wood very cheaply. Hastening back with these purchases, she rang at the house again. But to her surprise the old woman, who came grumbling to answer the bell, said that her mother had since gone out.

"No, I don't know where she was bound," she told Miranda querulously. "Sometimes she wanders in and out all day, and often as not forgets to take her latchkey—as if I hadn't bother enough, without minding the door for folk behind in their rent." She eyed Miranda's basket shrewdly. "Happen you can pay me something yourself, miss, as it seems you've come to look after her."

Miranda opened the purse and gave her a half crown. "That's all I can spare just now," she said, "but I'll see you have more as soon as we're put to rights." Then she went back upstairs to kindle a fire and set the kettle to boil.

The chill was off the room by the time her mother came home. Sitting her down beside the hearth, Miranda quickly brewed a pot of tea, and poured them each a brimming cupful. "Drink that up now," she said firmly. "It'll warm you for a start, and I'll boil the eggs and toast some bread in the meantime."

Her mother sipped the tea obediently; but after drinking only half of it, she handed the cup back. "I can't take anything more just now, dear," she said. "It's very kind of you, though." And tears came into her eyes.

"Never mind, then, Mother," Miranda said. "I'll bring you something later on. But where did you go out to? You oughtn't to have left without telling me."

"I only went for a stroll," her mother replied vaguely. "Now and then I feel I can't stop inside a moment longer, and I walk about the streets, just to relieve my feelings."

"Well, you're not to go off that way again," Miranda told her. "Besides, you should be resting in bed until you're stronger. Come along, I'll tidy the covers and back you go."

Her mother submitted to these ministrations, and soon fell asleep; while Miranda, sitting down to her own breakfast, tried to think how they were to go on. There was barely money enough to keep them warmed and fed for another week, and even the sale of her mother's ring and chain could mean only a certain respite before they found themselves penniless once more. Yet Miranda herself was unfit to earn their living. Apart from making baskets, she possessed no other skill; nor would she have dared leave her mother alone all day, even if she could have found work of the most menial kind. Once again, she regretted her earlier failures; for she might at least have taken in mending, had she learned to sew properly before.

Then she wondered a little about that—remembering her unexpected mastery of the baskets. Was it possible that her fingers were still endowed with their former magic? And if so, might they not prove adept at sewing as well? She sat very quiet for a few moments; and then, jumping to her feet, hastened downstairs and knocked at the old woman's door.

"If you please, may I borrow a needle and thread?" Miranda asked when she appeared.

"Eh, what next?" the old woman muttered impatiently; but she withdrew, and came back with a needle and a reel of cotton. "Mind you return them before the day's out," she said, shutting the door with a bang.

Once upstairs again, Miranda removed her shawl from its hook behind the door and began to look it over, recalling that the worn flannel, already patched and darned so extensively, had by now given way in one or two places further. Then, threading her needle, she began with some trepidation to stitch the ragged edges together.

She worked slowly, scarcely daring to breathe. Yet somehow she found herself guiding the needle in a singularly artful fashion—so that bit by bit the cloth was woven up again, nearly as good as new. Though even while she sewed Miranda could hardly believe that she did this work herself; it was as if she watched her fingers in a dream, and the magic they performed might have belonged to the needle, or the shawl, rather than to any skill of her own.

But at last, breaking off the thread, she laid down her work with a sigh of triumph and relief. Her mother still slept, and it appeared safe to go out for a time; so she threw the shawl about her shoulders and silently left the room.

Having returned the needle and spool to the old woman, who looked much astonished to see them again so soon, Miranda walked along to the next street and bravely entered a dressmaker's establishment often patronized by both her mother and her aunt.

At first, having offered her services to its rather formidable proprietress, she met with only a skeptical frown. But after Miranda had pointed out the flawless mending in her shawl, and given her aunt's and mother's names as references, there was a marked change in the dressmaker's manner; so that almost before she knew it, Miranda found herself engaged—on a piecework basis, to be sure—to take home a number of shirts and underlinens left at the shop for fine repair.

In addition, she was lent a small workbasket containing needles and a scissors and several spools of cotton, all of the best quality. "There's many a job of mending spoilt by a dull needle, or a thread too coarse," the dressmaker asserted. "Though we shan't put up with the least carelessness, mind. You'll be dismissed if anything comes back less than perfect."

"Yes, ma'am, I'll do my best," Miranda replied meekly. But she went home in a state of elation, to inform her mother that their living was assured for the present and they need not turn to her aunt for help.

Her mother received this news with surprising composure, apparently quite content to let her daughter earn their bread, as well as seeming entirely to have forgotten Miranda's futile attempts at stitchery in the past. Moreover, when Miranda's aunt came to call the next afternoon, her visit also proved less difficult than might have been expected.

For, insisting that her aunt be admitted to the room, Miranda simply explained that she had found employment, and wished to look after her mother herself. While her aunt was patently shocked by the idea of her niece's taking in mending, Miranda stood firm; and even her mother, who had at first shrunk back, came forward in the end and asked, with perfect dignity, that some additional clothing be sent round to them there. Miranda's aunt could only agree to this request, and took her leave soon afterwards, shaking her head over the whole business.

From that time on, Miranda's mother appeared largely relieved of her former obsessions. Yet, while she was more at peace, her mind tended to wander. She would often talk about events of the past as if they had just occurred, or fail to recall some incident of the week before; and in spite of being made to rest and take proper nourishment, she continued weak and ill, passing entire days confined to her bed—although on other occasions she rose and dressed herself, and would have gone out, regardless of the hour or the weather, had not Miranda dissuaded her.

On the whole, however, they led a life of sufficient tranquillity, with Miranda stitching beside the fire, and her mother settled in bed, rambling on about the years when she had been mistress of her own house. She frequently spoke of Miranda's father now, and appeared to have forgotten that Miranda had ever won his disfavor or been estranged from her parents. Then, one morning, out of the blue, she remarked how pleasant it would be when Miranda was married at last, and they could take up residence in her husband's house with its numerous servants and luxurious appointments.

"But, Mother," Miranda answered her, startled, "surely you must remember that I wasn't to be married, after all."

"Oh, that was just an unfortunate misunderstanding," declared her mother serenely. "And then there was your father's death that stood in the way—for of course you weren't free to marry while we were still in mourning. But time enough's passed by now, and there's no reason the wedding can't take place as soon as you like."

"No, Mother," Miranda said gently, "I'm afraid there's to be no wedding. You mustn't get such a notion into your head, you'll only be disappointed."

Nevertheless, her mother remained convinced that Miranda's marriage was imminent, and began to look upon her daily sewing as the preparation of linens for her new home. Even when Miranda showed her over and over that she was only mending shirts and petticoats, she could not dispel these vain hopes; and in the end found it easier to humor her mother's fancies, putting off her repeated questions about the wedding with an indefinite reply.

Then, one rainy afternoon late in the spring, when Miranda had left her mother asleep and gone out through a downpour to return her day's mending to the dress-

(155)

maker's, she came home to find the room empty, although her mother's shawl was hanging from its customary hook.

Running downstairs again, she looked out the door, but her mother was nowhere in sight, and the rain fell heavily still. So she waited in the shelter of the doorway, until, after a quarter of an hour, she saw her mother coming along the street, her clothing drenched, and sodden strands of hair dripping about her shoulders.

"How could you be so foolish, Mother?" Miranda scolded, leading her into the house. "To go out in such weather, and without a shawl? You'll take cold, for certain."

Her mother merely smiled. "I'm perfectly all right, dear," she said. "I don't mind a bit of wet. You see, it occurred to me that I hadn't got you a wedding gift, so I thought I'd just run out and buy one. But when I was nearly to the shop, I found I'd forgotten my purse. Wasn't that silly of me? But I'll go another day, instead," she said placidly, "there's time enough, I expect. When did you say the wedding was to be?"

"Never mind the wedding now," Miranda replied in exasperation. "You're to go straight to bed and stay there."

Back in their room, she dried her mother's hair, and helped her out of her wet things and into a nightdress. Then, tucking her into bed, she boiled the kettle and brought her a steaming cup of tea. But despite Miranda's precautions, during the evening her mother developed a hoarse cough that racked her thin body and left her laboring for breath. Miranda watched beside her through the night, helping her to sit up each time another bout of coughing seized her; but by morning she was worse, too weak to stir, and so feverish that she scarcely recognized her daughter or the room in which she lay.

Greatly alarmed, Miranda hurried down into the street. She ran all the way to the apothecary's shop, and rang the bell again and again, as it was too early for anyone to be downstairs. Finally, her aunt appeared, much surprised to see her niece at the door. But on hearing what was the matter, she drew Miranda inside, and called up the stairs for James to go in haste and fetch the doctor.

"It's just how your father was stricken," she said to Miranda in ominous tones, after James, looking sleepy and disgruntled, had set forth on his errand with no more than a passing nod at his cousin. "He took a chill, and it turned to a cough, and in three days' time he was gone."

But Miranda scarcely attended, so impatient was she to be off again; and when at last the doctor arrived, she led him without delay to her mother's room, where the poor woman now lay moaning and nearly unconscious.

The doctor managed to administer a spoonful of medicine; but afterwards he shook his head gravely. "I won't deceive you," he said. "The fever's got out of hand, and she simply hasn't the strength to throw it off. You'd better try cold applications—but unless there's a change soon, I doubt that she'll survive another day."

Miranda looked at him in dread. "Isn't there some other medicine she could have?" she asked.

"None that would be of any use to her now," he replied. "I'll call again this afternoon, and we'll hope for the best; but I wouldn't want to offer you false encouragement."

When the doctor had gone, Miranda wrung out a cloth in cold water and, having sponged her mother's face and arms, laid it over her brow. She appeared quieter, although her breath now came in shallow gasps, and sometimes halted for so long a time that Miranda feared the worst.

Then, as she bent over to remove the cloth and wring it out afresh, she heard her mother murmur a word or two.

"What is it, Mother?" she inquired anxiously. "Is there something I can do?"

"Your wedding gift," her mother whispered. "I would have bought one, but I didn't have the money with me."

"Never mind that now," Miranda said soothingly. "There's no need to fret about it today."

"No, Miranda," her mother said, opening her eyes, her voice faint but distinct. "Listen to me, dear. I want you to have my ring and my chain—they're all I've got left. I fear I won't see you married, but at least you'll know that I thought of you."

"Of course I will, Mother," Miranda said, her sight suddenly veiled by tears.

"Take them off me, child—I want to see you wearing them," she demanded feebly. So Miranda unfastened the gold chain from her mother's neck, and slipped the ring, with its clear green stone, from her finger; and put them on herself.

"There," her mother sighed. "That's all right, then."

With these words she was overcome by another paroxysm of coughing, which shook her wasted body so grievously that Miranda could not bear to watch, and hid her face in her hands.

And when she looked up again, her mother's eyes had grown vacant, and she had ceased altogether to breathe.

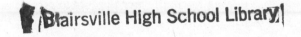

iranda's aunt insisted on paying the doctor's fee, as well as the cost of the funeral. "We couldn't see your mother buried like a pauper, could we, dear?" she said to Miranda. "And I know you've no money to speak of yourself. Besides, now that she's gone, poor soul, you'd far better come and live as one of the family again. It's most unsuitable for you to continue working as a common seamstress—and for my own dressmaker, at that."

Miranda, however, was by no means ready to give up her independent livelihood. She felt sure that her mother would not have wished it; and she herself was wholly repelled by the prospect of living at such close quarters with her aunt, who might never say in so many words that Miranda had brought her parents to grief, but whose air of self-righteousness seemed to accuse her just as clearly. Therefore, Miranda replied that she had rather stay as she was, for the present; and although her aunt was considerably annoyed, there was little she could say, except that she thought Miranda very willful and wrongheaded.

Yet, in truth, Miranda judged herself even more harshly than her aunt might have done, as with every day she grew the more deeply convinced that she was now to blame for her mother's death as well as her father's. Hour after hour she stitched alone, plagued by bitter regrets. Nor was she freed from them when, unable to bear the silence of that grim little room any longer, she laid aside her work and went out to walk aimlessly about the streets; for, although she sometimes found that her wanderings led her back to the market square, Miranda no longer cherished the slightest hope of seeing the gypsies again.

She had been given scant opportunity to think of them while she was so much absorbed in looking after her mother; though her sleep had been haunted by one persistent dream, wherein she pursued over an endless, dusky heath a figure bearing a lantern—a figure elusive as quicksilver, now Leo's, now Bella's, now that of some indeterminate stranger, who fled before her like a glimmering will-o'-the-wisp, while she strove with leaden feet to reach its side.

But by this time, even to her waking mind, the gypsies had faded away to little more than ghostly fabrications, as insubstantial as the pictures in her old storybook. What were Bella's cards, in the end, but bits of illustrated pasteboard, no less deceptive than the pretty images that had played her false before? Besides, regardless of anything those cards had foretold, Miranda felt she could never again, in good conscience, go off with the gypsies—for was it not her earlier flight which had led to her parents' ruin? Then how could she be so base as to follow that faithless course a second time?

Thus she brooded, day after day, while summer came and flourished and waned, and the whistled songs of birds nesting in the high house eaves gave way to plaintive cries of geese winging away before the autumn frosts.

But Miranda's solitary penance continued without change, except that her face in the glass looked increasingly thin and ashen. She took a certain dismal satisfaction in neglecting to eat, or to comb her hair, or to care for her clothes, while attending dutifully to the repair of others'; though on occasion she noticed this carelessness reflected in her work as well, discovering it so poorly done that she was obliged to snip out the stitches and begin over again.

Even so, in spite of every effort, her fingers seemed slowly to be losing their skill, and she found it more and more difficult to accomplish the simplest task of mending. One day, in fact, the dressmaker pointed out that none of the articles Miranda had returned was acceptably finished. "If this sort of thing continues, I shan't be able to keep you on," she admonished her. "I can't think what's come over you—your work was never at fault before."

Miranda attempted no excuse, but taking the garments back again went home to try to put them right. Yet not only did her fingers prove clumsier than ever, but her sight grew blurred at the close work; and after an hour's fruitless labor, she pushed the linens to one side of the table and sat staring before her in utter despair. For, unless she could somehow bring herself to sell her mother's ring and chain, and even those precious keepsakes given her by Leo and Bella and Nan, it appeared that she must swallow her pride at last, and accept the ignominious role of poor relation in her aunt's household.

Rising from her chair, she walked about the room, wringing her hands in a fever of indecision and distress.

But after a time she sat down again; and taking off her mother's ring, and Leo's, and her mother's chain from about her neck, and Nan's brooch from its place over her heart, she laid them in a little heap on the table before her.

Then, almost as an afterthought, she reached up to unfasten the gold hoops from her ears. As she did so, however, there came into her mind something Bella had said on presenting her with those earrings—something about gypsy gold, given in trust, and not to be lightly worn.

And in that moment Miranda realized that she could no more sacrifice any one of these cherished tokens than sell her own head, or her hands, or her heart. They might be only inanimate trinkets, mere elements of metal and stone; yet all were grown as vital to her as the living tissues they threaded or circled or spanned: as vital to her as those for whom she wore them, whose lives were fused with the innermost substance of her soul.

Then surely she might endure her aunt's odious charity, if it meant remaining at one with those she had loved; and if she must humble herself by doing so, that humility should serve as a fit and abiding atonement.

Gathering up her treasures from the table again, Miranda restored each one to its rightful place. And afterwards, in sober acquiescence, she put on her shawl, and began to assemble the things she must take away with her—the pile of linens, some clothing of her mother's, and Dulcie's basket, empty of all but her mother's purse.

And she also found, on the cluttered mantelshelf, her discarded kerchief, long ago tied about certain articles for their safekeeping: one or two small remembrances given her by the gypsies; her bottle of walnut brew, its dregs turned cloudy with age; and Bella's cards, left there nearly forgotten these many months. Or perhaps not so much forgotten as avoided; for now, when she took down the kerchief, she felt strangely reluctant to look on its contents again.

Nevertheless, by way of making some amends, she untied it, and, removing the cards from their own wrappings, pensively shuffled them up in her hands, although she had neither the heart nor the curiosity to lay them out as she might have done. She merely sighed and, fitting the pack together, began to wrap the silken cloth about it once more.

Her hands remained awkward, however, and a few cards slipped aside and fell to the floor. Stooping to retrieve them, she found one fallen face up—and recognized, with a start, the familiar card of the Fool, who seemed to look at her, laughing, even now.

Though inclined to dismiss the matter as a coincidence, she picked up the others, turning them over as well. And to her increasing wonder, she saw that the first was the Nine of Swords, the card of misery and bereavement; the second, Temperance, the card of patience and frugality, whose winged figure poured the waters of life from one vessel into another; while upon the third a jubilant woman, perhaps the High Priestess herself, danced naked, encircled by a garland of flourishing leaves: and this was the last and highest of all the pack, the card of the World, whose meaning was truth unveiled, and sublime fulfillment.

Spreading out all four cards on the table, Miranda stared at them awestruck. For they contained the veritable pattern of her life; nor could she doubt them any longer, not even that final joyful card of the World.

As she sat gazing in silence upon this wonderful card, Miranda's eyes filled with tears. No more the blinding tears of anger or grief or despair, but tears distilled from a curious bliss of surrender and triumph, yearning and gratitude, bewilderment and comprehension, refined to a single spirit, exquisitely clear, yet also subtly mercurial: an elixir as deeply mysterious, as brimming with revelation, as the fathomless springs of life, or the changeless flux of the sea—or that limpid orb of crystal held obscure in the shadows of Bella's cupboard.

Obscure, but a presence nonetheless, in the marvelous waters of these tears: as slowly they seemed to be gathered and rounded before Miranda's eyes into an equally perfect orb, a crystal at whose heart sprang up, like a brilliant flame, that same exalted figure of the World; and now, while it danced, this apparition laughed, with the mingled sounds of every laughter Miranda had known in the past—the sea's, and Death's, and a multitude of others', even her own; and woven among the rest, yet also risen above them in exultation, the Fool's.

As though the Fool had laughed hidden in each, dancing his way through a host of scattered identities, assuming the hues and features of every disparate guise. But here, at the end of his wanderings, he danced in the World's embrace; and the World resolved his motley facets into her flawless golden fire, so that the two of them danced as a single figure: whose truth was neither that of light nor darkness, heaven nor earth, but simply that of its dancing; and whose dance was itself the all-encompassing image of truth.

Truth, an image of perfect completion, marrying earth and heaven into a seamless whole. Truth, within whose vast encircling sphere even folly and wisdom danced wedded together, a figure of consummate symmetry—a figure, indeed, *both foolish and wise at once.*

Like a burst of music attendant upon that miraculous wedding, Bella's words sang out in Miranda's head; and struck by their ultimate sense, she laughed aloud. For they celebrated the marriage of her own diverse identities and disguises, pronouncing her base and noble, clumsy and skillful, blind and blessed with the gift of sight: as these were but the separate stuffs and scraps composing her final truth, which was fashioned whole and immaculate out of its muddle of shining threads and dappled patches.

And thus arrayed in the clarity of that patched and radiant garment—hers to be worn as simply as her elemental flesh and blood and bone, with neither fear nor illusion, vanity nor shame—Miranda emerged from her long season of mourning, made one with herself, and reconciled to all: even the guilts and sorrows of the shadowy little cell in which she sat, as, laughing, she awoke to it again, her ordinary sight restored.

Though this sight was now as lucid as her vision of the moment before; for these, like the Fool and the World, were themselves made whole and one.

Miranda sat quietly for a time, filled with a greater peace than ever she had known. But presently she got up and put away the cards; and having tidied her hair before the glass, gathered together her various possessions. She made a neat bundle of her mother's clothing, another of the dressmaker's linens, and packing everything else into Dulcie's basket, looked about the room in a silent gesture of farewell. Then she went away, and left it behind.

topping first to pay the old woman her final rent, and next delivering the linens and workbasket to the dressmaker's, where she told the proprietress that she would be unable to take home any further mending, Miranda turned her steps towards the apothecary's shop.

She entered without hesitation, and calmly requested her cousin, who stood behind the counter working with a mortar and pestle, to summon his mother, as she had something to say to her. James, surveying Miranda with ill-concealed disdain, put aside his work to deliver this message; and returning, said that his mother was engaged at the moment but would come down presently if Miranda cared to wait.

So Miranda stood to one side, while her cousin paid her little further heed and was, at all events, soon occupied with a woman who came in to have a bottle of medicine refilled.

Still Miranda waited, and her aunt did not appear. She diverted herself meanwhile by looking over the impressive display of glass jars and flasks set out along the counter—though most of them, Miranda well knew, held nothing but colored water. Yet, as her glance fell idly on one of these vessels, its contents dyed to a deep shade of blue, she seemed to glimpse some flickering light reflected at its center, like that of a faint spark or a distant star. As she looked more closely, this glimmering grew brighter, and waxed further, until it appeared to take on a tenuous form, silvery-pale, but shining nonetheless. And slowly its image was formed into a face, which she recognized as her mother's: pale as bone, but at the same time radiant, starlike, even now.

There was nothing in the least fearsome about it. For unlike that deathly face of her father's she had seen in the crystal, this one craved no awful pity, instead appearing to offer her a compassion of its own. Though gradually the face was altered, and she saw it to be her mother's no longer, but Nan's, pale, like the other, though dimmed in brilliance, its features wasted and drawn; and she seemed also to hear Nan's voice, except that it was Bella's as well —as if the two of them called her at once, by both her names: *Miranda, Mira.*

Then Nan's voice, and her face, faded away, until there remained only the clear blue depths of those waters, and Bella's voice alone, calling from a distance ever more profound, *Mira, Mira, listen!* And still more faintly, *Listen!*

Whereafter, although she strained to recapture some trace of it, nothing further came to her ears, save for the sound of James's customer speaking nearby.

"It's been a wonder," the woman was saying, while James wrapped up her purchase in brown paper. "My daughter's felt that much better in just the fortnight she's been taking it—her fever's gone, and she's out of bed every day. When I think how weak she'd grown—wasting away she was, and sometimes her head aching so you hardly dared speak to her—why, it's like a miracle! If only we'd gone to the doctor about it before—but you see, every few days she'd seem to recover, and we'd keep hoping the worst was past. Ah, well, better late than never," she added, with a laugh. "There's your money. Costly stuff, isn't it? And bitter as gall, she tells me. But worth the price, to be sure." And placing a coin in James's hand, the woman received her parcel and went away.

Miranda moved along the counter towards her cousin, scarcely able to believe her ears. "James," she asked in awed tones, "what medicine was it you sold that woman?"

Her cousin looked at her in surprise. "It's a remedy for the ague, made from a foreign bark," he told her loftily. "Your father always kept some on hand, though there's not much call for it hereabouts. Still, you see a case now and again. Why do you ask?"

"I know of somebody who's ill, in just the way that woman described," Miranda replied slowly. "It's a pity I can't take her some of that medicine."

James, with a pointed glance at Miranda's shabby clothing, smiled condescendingly. "Yes, you'd want money to do that," he said, "and I don't suppose you've a sovereign in your pocket to spare."

Miranda stared at him, thunderstruck. "No, I haven't," she said. "But I believe I know someone who has!"

Before her cousin's astonished eyes, she set down her bundle and her basket upon the counter and, without another word, turned and ran out of the shop.

It was by now late in the afternoon, and though the sun shone brightly still, there was an edge of frost to the air; but Miranda's heart beat fast, and she felt not the slightest cold as she hastened along towards the marketplace.

The market was busy again with its weekly stalls, and she was obliged to push her way through the crowd. But at last, at the far side of the square, she saw, as she had somehow known she must find them, the same three figures who had stood there so long ago: Dulcie, and Leo, and Jemmy, waiting together beside their familiar barrow.

She ran up to them, and threw herself into Dulcie's arms, and then into Leo's, and even caught Jemmy in an awkward embrace before he ducked away.

"I was sure you'd be here!" she cried, laughing and nearly weeping at the same time. "It was Bella's doing—she as much as sent for me herself."

Dulcie and Leo stopped short in the midst of their joyful greetings, and looked at one another in dismay.

"It was Bella who told us to come for you," Dulcie said gently. "But I've sorry news for you, dear. Bella died, just over a week ago."

"Oh, Dulcie," Miranda gasped, stricken. "How could she have died? She never seemed ill, or even so very old."

"Ah, she was older than you might have thought," Dulcie replied. "But she wasn't ill for long, only a day or two, when she didn't get up. And the end came quietly in the night, while she was asleep."

"Oh, dear Bella," Miranda mourned, her jubilant spirits dashed. "I'd so longed to see her again, and I'd so much to say to her."

"Well, she's brought us together all the same," said Dulcie. "It was when she first took to her bed, she told Tom we must pack up and come this way again. She said when we got here I was to bring Leo and Jemmy and look for you in the market, and you'd soon find us if we came every day—though we've only come today for the first time, haven't we, Leo?"

Leo merely grinned; but he held tight to Miranda's hand, as though he would never release it again.

"But how is Nan faring, now that Bella's gone?" Miranda asked, recalling Nan's face in her vision, and suddenly afraid.

"I've been looking after her myself," Dulcie replied, "though she's never got out of bed since. She seems to have lost strength; but I've no doubt she'll be the better for seeing you again."

"But do you know, Dulcie, it was really on Nan's account that I came here," Miranda exclaimed. "I saw something about her, though Bella came into it, too— only then it turned out to be a woman in the shop, talking about some medicine that sounded the very thing for Nan."

Dulcie and Leo appeared slightly bewildered. But Jemmy, who had been standing by with his hands in his pockets, whistling softly to himself, looked straight at Miranda. "Shall I give you the coin now?" he asked.

"Why, Jemmy, how ever did you know I'd want it?" Miranda asked in surprise.

"She said you would," he answered matter-of-factly. And he drew from his pocket Miranda's handkerchief, frayed and begrimed, but with the coin knotted fast at its center.

"That's Bella he means," Dulcie explained. "She sent for him the day before she died, though I never knew what she said."

"You can have the handkerchief, too," Jemmy offered. "Leo said he'd take me after live rabbits one day soon, didn't you, Leo?"

Leo laughed, and gave him a friendly cuff. Miranda herself smiled at last, and began to unfasten the gold sovereign from its tattered wrappings. "I'm sorry you've got to give it up," she said to Jemmy.

"I don't mind," the boy replied, returning his empty hands to his pockets. "I'm too old for toys now. And Tom's taught me to whistle, Miranda—did you hear?" Upon which he gave out a piercing note to prove it.

Dulcie said that was quite enough, and the boy subsided, though he continued whistling under his breath, his eyes on Miranda.

"I'll go back this minute and get my things," she told them eagerly. "Will you wait for me here?"

Of course they agreed. So Miranda retraced her steps through the market, and then ran back to the shop. She arrived flushed and breathless, to find James and her aunt standing in conversation over her basket and bundle.

"Why, Miranda, wherever did you go off to?" said her aunt, looking up reproachfully as she entered. "James said you'd asked to see me, but when I came down you'd left without a word."

"I'm sorry, Aunt, but I've no time to explain," Miranda replied, and turned to James instead. "I'd like a bottle of that medicine we were talking about, please," she said to him, "and write out the proper dose on the label—as quick as you can! Here's the money—you said a sovereign, didn't you?"

She held out the coin on her palm, to James's manifest amazement. But as Miranda urged him again to make haste, he went behind the counter, and before long had filled another bottle and labeled it accordingly.

Meanwhile, Miranda's aunt drew herself up and demanded an explanation of her niece's behavior. Miranda only smiled, and said that she needn't worry about her any longer, since she was going back to the gypsies, this time to stay. "And I believe I'll take these things of Mother's with me," she added reflectively. "There's good stuff in them yet, and I daresay they'll be of some use—perhaps even to make me a wedding dress."

Remarking her aunt's baffled expression, she laughed and put out her hand, where her mother's ring, catching the light, winked and glinted. "Don't fret over me, Aunt," she said. "All's well, and I don't bear you any grudge, nor James either. Indeed, you're welcome to this house—I'd far sooner live in a caravan, myself."

Then, as James and his mother looked on speechless, Miranda tucked the bottle of medicine into her basket, and the bundle of clothes under her arm; and bidding them both farewell, took her leave of the shop forever.

The sun was setting by the time she reached the market again. The crowds had thinned, and some of the stalls were being taken down. But the three gypsies stood there waiting; and at Miranda's approach, Jemmy greeted her with a bolder whistle than ever—which, shrill though it was, resounded in her ears with a music as sweet as ever Tom's fiddle had played.

Before they made ready to leave, however, Miranda told Dulcie she had something to give her; and taking off her mother's gold chain, she fastened it about Dulcie's neck. "My mother died, in the spring," she said quietly. "And I'd like you to wear this, that was hers, as a bond between the two of you."

Dulcie looked uncomfortable, saying that of course she would be happy to wear it, but was very sorry about Miranda's mother. "For you know I never meant to take you away from her," she murmured.

"No, Dulcie," Miranda replied. "It was the other way round. You taught me how to be a good daughter, and so did Rosa, and Tom, and everyone; and I'm sure she'd only be grateful."

Then Leo, who had stood for some time regarding Miranda with a curious expression, set his hand lightly on the crown of her head. "You've left off your kerchief, I see," he said, half teasing, yet with a faint anxiety as well. "Nobody'd take you for a gypsy now, Miranda, with that hair—and what's become of your gypsy skin, for that matter?"

"I've no need of them any longer, have I?" returned Miranda with a smile. "Though I'll always wear Bella's earrings—and where are yours, I'd like to know, if you're so much a gypsy yourself?"

"Ah, I see how it's to be," Leo said, grinning. "You're thinking you'll talk me round to some, once we're wed, isn't it? Well, we'll just see about that."

"Nay, Leo, I was only joking," Miranda said quickly. "I'd not have you other than you are, for all the gold in the world."

Leo, embarrassed, tousled her hair in reply; whereupon Miranda gave him a push, and they both laughed. Until Dulcie, in mock admonition, told them to leave that skylarking and help her to pack up the barrow so they could be on their way.

When everything was in order, the four of them set off at last. But this time, unlike that frosty night a year ago, Miranda walked at Leo's side as he pushed the barrow along the cobbled streets leading away from the town: away towards that cold and starlit field where the caravans stood about a flickering fire, and the other gypsies waited to welcome them home.